SOAP ON A ROPE

COLD CREAM MURDERS - BOOK 3

BARBARA SILKSTONE

Soap on a Rope©

Cold Cream Murders - Book 3

Barbara Silkstone 2019

BARBARA SILKSTONE NEWS LETTER

To receive an email when a new book by Barbara Silkstone is published, or for special sales and giveaways please sign up for my newsletter. Your information will not be shared with anyone and you may unsubscribe at any time. I promise not to pester you!

With love & laughter!

http://secondactcafe.com/barbara-silkstone/

COLD CREAM MURDERS

Olive Peroni put out her family therapy shingle six years ago never thinking her top client would be the retired head of a New York crime family. When Olive's Nonna dies, leaves her a condo in Florida and a secret recipe for miracle cold cream, she grabs the chance at a new life in Starfish Cove, Florida, making designer creams for ladies who spend far too much time at the beach. Business is brisk and life is good! Olive even makes a wild new best friend and business partner in Lizzy, the real estate agent who handles the transfer of Nonna's condo.

But when the quiet little community on the Gulf of Mexico soon begins to compete with a certain notorious coastal village in Maine, Olive finds herself solving odd-ball murders as often as she soothes wrinkles. Clean and wholesome!

Each book contains a recipe for homemade cosmetics and beautifiers!

SOAP ON A ROPE BLURB

SOAP ON A ROPE – COLD CREAM MURDERS – Book 3

When Nelson Dingler is found dangling from a chandelier—feet-side up—Grams Dingler determines to find her son's killer. Can Olive help her best friend save her feisty grandmother from suffering the same fate? And can the Cold Cream Shop survive while Olive psyches out the killer?

Contains a recipe for heavenly lavender lemon honey soap.

CHAPTER 1

*S*ophia Napoli stood in perfect dancer's posture at her marble-top kitchen counter. With her tall frame erect and her shoulders back, she wiggled her voluptuous bottom—moving to the samba music playing softly throughout her palatial tower residence on Biscayne Bay.

The Italian film star's technique for chopping green peppers into fine little cubes would have put the greatest chef to shame. Using the blade of her knife, she scooped the peppers aside into a little pile, and then attacked a peeled onion. When her eyes began to moisten, she ran the onion under tap water, and continued to slice.

Lizzy and I sat at the opposite end of the sleek counter our mouths hanging open—not from hunger but from awe. How easily life can turn a corner and offer up the wildest surprises.

After I met Lizzy Kelly my world topsy-turvyed into one astonishment after another. The combination of our energies nudged me to take my foot off the brakes and swerve into the bumper car lane of life. I morphed from on-call mobster therapist to cold cream entrepreneur and crime solver in the course of a few wild days and, incredibly, the pace over the next months accelerated from there.

Sophia paused in her little dance. "This brings me such joy—making my special omelets for the sleuth ladies of Starfish Cove!" Using a graceful pick and crack rhythm Sophia broke half a dozen eggs into a large clear bowl, never dropping a shell or dribbling goop. She beat them with a whisk while chatting with us.

"Almost forgot funghi!" She plucked a handful of porcini from a colander and began to slice.

"Chopping gives the most pleasure in cooking. There is such passion in axing—no?" She smiled broadly. There were so many layers to this woman. So much more than beauty and international stardom—she was down-to-earth and funny.

I grinned back at her. "I know what you mean. Now and then it feels good to slam something really hard."

From behind Sophia's shoulder, a beam of sunlight bounced off the green-blue waters of Biscayne Bay, shot through the tinted glass that ran floor to ceiling, reflected off the pedestaled gold statue—her Oscar—and pierced my eyes. I angled my barstool out of the assaulting sunlight and returned to watching our hostess.

She scooped all the sliced goodies, including minced basil into a bowl and then wiggle-walked to the stove. She had Lizzy beat in the hubba-hubba saunter competition.

The wonder on my partner's face tickled me. The first day we met she confessed her adoration for the Italian movie star after admiring my grandmother's collection of photographs and portraits of her beloved Sophia Napoli. Next to pizza, the woman was Italy's most famous ambassador.

"I can hear your nonna laughing in heaven," Sophia said. "Her thoughtful little present to me bring us together." With an elegant motion she poured green-gold olive oil into a white enamel skillet.

She opened her hand in my direction. "Though we never met, I was sad to see Isabella's obituary. At least ten years ago she sent me a lifetime subscription to the *Silverfish Gazette*. Out of the blue! Like that!" She snapped her fingers. "It comes in the mail with a note she is from my village in Italy and hopes the small-town gossip reminds me of home. I send her a thank-you card, but never kept in touch. Colpa mia."

So *that* was how Sophia Napoli came to subscribe to the *Silverfish Gazette*. I sat mesmerized by all that happened since we left the airport, chauffeured by Sophia's hunky assistant and bodyguard, Fabio Santoro.

She adjusted the flame under the skillet. "Isabella was right. The news, she comforts me, even though I was just a girl when my mother brought me to America. I always have the *Silverfish* when I travel. I read the stories from Starfish Cove over and over and they soothe me. When my life is too crazy, the *Silverfish* reminds me there are places where people are happy to live small lives."

She tumbled the chopped vegetables into the oil and gave them a gentle stir.

"Then I read of the murders! What happened to my innocent town? And then your name, Olive Peroni! A relative of Isabella— we must meet the next time I'm in Florida! You and sweet Lizzy are heroes—heroines. See the story of your bravery is on the counter."

I reached for the old issue of the *Silverfish Gazette*, the grainy photo of Lizzy and me above the fold but below the paper's slogan *Catch the News Before It Crawls Away!*

The way Lizzy's grandmother—known to everyone as Grams— recounted our most recent case one would think Lizzy and I wore bodysuits adorned with a gigantic **S** on the chest and flaring capes of red satin.

It was the first time I'd taken a good look at the small print on the irregular little paper. *Circulation 100,000.* Grams was the *Silverfish's* ace reporter in charge of exaggeration. The beachside community of Starfish Cove had a population that might stretch to fifteen hundred if you included the cats and dogs.

A small block ad on the lower left corner of the front page caught my eye. I hadn't paid attention to the flip side except to check the spelling on our *Open House* invitation ad.

"Lizzy, did you notice this?" I pointed to the black and red box with a magician's hat. Offbeat even for Starfish Cove.

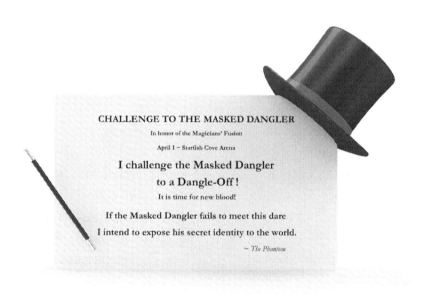

CHALLENGE TO THE MASKED DANGLER

In honor of the Magicians' Fusion

April 1 ~ Starfish Cove Arena

I challenge the Masked Dangler

to a Dangle-Off !

It is time for new blood!

If the Masked Dangler fails to meet this dare

I intend to expose his secret identity to the world.

~ *The Phantom*

Stretching across the counter Lizzy snaked the *Gazette* her way. "Oh no. He's back."

CHAPTER 2

*S*ophia ceased humming and stopped her wiggle-dance. "Che cosa?"

"Nothing!" Lizzy said. "Just some silly pretend magicians—a cheesy way of getting attention for their convention. Trust me, you're not missing anything. When you come to visit, we'll show you the beauty of the beaches. Did I mention I have fifty-two finches in my home? They fly loose all over my house. My dog is named WonderDog. He adores the little birds and wears them in his long stringy hair."

"Your life is like a fairytale—no?"

This visit was the fairytale. Two cold cream mini-moguls from the west coast of Florida being omeleted by an international film star on the twenty-second-floor of Rocca Garda, the most exclusive, high security building in Miami.

Sophia went back to cooking. "Presto! Presto! No one leaves my house without a full stomaco! You will have time to make your return flight. But you must come again and stay longer. And someday I will visit Starfish Cove. I fly to London tomorrow for the young prince's celebration and then to Switzerland. I am always busy but I come to visit Isabella's beloved town by the sea."

Lizzy successfully diverted attention from the ad. Why?

With the edge of her spatula, Sophia cut the giant omelet into thirds, then expertly used it to slide the pieces onto gleaming china plates, one for each of us. "Mangia! Mangia! Eat!"

I squinched my eyes shut and sent a telepathic message to Lizzy. *Please Lizzy don't ask for ketchup.*

"Do you have ketchup?"

Sophia's lower jaw dropped an inch. My partner had just insulted the labors of a legend. I glared at my ketchup-loving friend, but she was clueless.

Our hostess burst in to laughter. "I don't think there is what you call *ketchup* in this entire tower."

Lizzy waved her hand dismissively. "No problem. This is wonderful."

Fortunately for Lizzy's shin the position of my barstool prevented me from giving her the good kick she deserved.

We tucked into our omelets. Between bites we answered Sophia's questions about our world and Nonna's cold cream.

"It would help your business if I endorse your cream. No?" Sophia's dark tiger-eyes flashed from me to Lizzy.

I almost choked on my omelet. "It would be fabulous but we can't afford an endorsement fee. Even if we give you a percentage of our sales, it won't amount to a thousandth or a millionth of what you should receive. You are known for not doing many endorsements."

"Fees? I didn't say anything about fees."

"But you have your image to protect! It would be presumptuous of me to think you would go out on a limb for us."

"Limbs are good! If you don't go out on the limb, you never learn to fly!" She grinned like a cat lapping a bowl of cream.

"I will send Fabio to Starfish Cove once I am with the royal family. I will not need his protection for the ten days I am in London or Switzerland. He will inspect your business, look at your bookkeeping, and test your beautifiers. If everything meets his approval, I will endorse."

She raised her hand and snapped her fingers. "If possible to be secret, I would enjoy time in Starfish Cove. But when I come I will disguise myself. Act as a relative. Yes?"

My phone rang from deep within my purse which sat on an antique table near the foyer. The loud ring was the one I'd assigned to Officer Kal Miranda. Torn between ignoring it and responding to the little twinge in my gut, I got up from the counter.

"Olive? This is a good plan. No?"

"It's a wonderful plan, Sophia! Excuse me while I grab my phone. That's an emergency ring."

We left Grams and Ivy in charge of the shop for the day. A tiny piece of my mind fretted over how things were going.

"Olive? It's Kal. Is Lizzy nearby?"

"She's not but hang on, I'll take the phone to her."

"Wait! We need to talk first!"

The tone in his voice chilled me.

"You should know this so you can comfort her. Nelson Dingler is dead."

"Lizzy's father?"

"Yes. *That* Nelson Dingler."

"Natural or unnatural?" I stepped further into the foyer so my voice wouldn't carry. It had been months since the last murder in Starfish Cove. We were overdue.

"The M.E. is saying natural by unnatural circumstances. Grams Dingler found the body when she went to check on her son. I'm worried about her. Can you ladies get an earlier flight?"

"We were about to leave for the airport. We land at five-fifteen."

"Meet me at Dingler's place. Now...put Lizzy on."

CHAPTER 3

*L*izzy pressed the phone to her ear. "Say that again." Confusion. Anger. Quivering lip.

Nelson Dingler, a larger than life figure, Commodore of the Starfish Cove Yacht Club. A bulldog. Often the centerpiece of gossip. Disliked by those who barely knew him. Hated by those who did.

I'd watched Lizzy wrangle, tangle, and seek his approval too many times to worry she might take his passing hard. He would not be missed except for the love she never felt and now stood no chance of ever winning.

She passed the phone back to me. "I should cry but I can't find the tears." She stepped away from the counter, walked to the glass wall overlooking the Bay and kept her back to us.

"Lizzy's father just passed away," I whispered to Sophia.

"Madre di Dio!" Sophia turned as if to follow Lizzy.

I reached out, touched her arm, and shook my head. "Give her a minute."

She mouthed the question *murder?*

Starfish Cove's reputation raced ahead of the facts. I whispered *no*—although I wasn't certain. What did natural by unnatural circumstances mean?

"I think it's best we leave right away. She'll want to be sure we're at the airport on time."

"I'll summon Fabio." She pressed a button on her watch. "Was sweet Lizzy close to her father?"

"Not at all. He was an angry man who did not like women."

She raised one brow.

As a trained psychologist, I knew Sophia would understand. I lowered my voice. "Not like that. He was a man who didn't like men *or* women but in particular he held no warmth for the ladies in his life. Lizzy spent a lot of her energy trying to win his approval. Now he's gone and she'll never succeed."

Sophia dabbed at her eyes with her napkin.

Lizzy returned and stood between us with dry eyes, her countenance not cheerful, but calm. "Don't look at me like you're worried. I'm fine. Can we leave now for the airport in case there's traffic?"

Fabio entered the room in response to the buzzer on Sophia's watch. "Yes, Ms. Napoli?"

The man moved like a jungle cat—muscular, sleek, and silent. He was easy on the eyes in that smoldering Italian way. My taste in men ran in my genes.

"The ladies must leave now. Make certain they get to the airport quickly." Sophia reached out and embraced Lizzy. "I'm sorry for your loss. You're a strong woman. Do what must be done. We shall meet again—soon."

Held in her motherly embrace Lizzy swallowed a sob. "Sorry to eat and run," she mumbled as she freed herself.

We left Sophia's in disarray. Life had just turned another of those sharp corners leaving happy street and headed for my monthly confab with the medical examiner. It was only a matter of time before the gossips linked me with the M.E. We had to stop meeting like this.

Lizzy and I sat silently in the back of Sophia's black sedan, the heavily tinted windows shutting out the world. Fabio occasionally peered at us in the rearview mirror as he maneuvered through the absurdly dense pre-rush hour traffic. We arrived at the airport with forty minutes to spare.

Sophia's bodyguard handed us out of the sedan. A security officer approached, glanced at the celebrity license plate, nodded once politely and waited while we stood outside the car thanking Fabio.

Once inside the terminal, we dashed to the gate, showed our boarding passes, and waited with our fellow passengers to be called.

'Tell me about the magician's challenge and why you steered the conversation away from it."

"It's uncomfortable to talk about." Lizzy hesitated but then began in almost a whisper. "Grams once shared a secret with me. It concerned a performance by the Masked Dangler."

Lizzy looked around as if afraid to be overheard. "She described a thin masked man in tights who performed in the Starfish Cove arena. It was sort of a high-wire act without the wire."

Lizzy's voice quivered. "Two women in black bodysuits strapped his ankles into a harness. The Masked Dangler was lifted by some sort of machine to the tippy top of the arena dome. He dangled there by his feet, head down, and arms spread wide."

"That could give you a killer headache." I still didn't get the connection.

"Grams said at that point in the act the masked man was to fold his body at the waist, grab his legs, and work his hands up to his ankles until he was upright holding onto the rope with one hand. Then he'd lean over and unfasten the bindings on his feet."

"And this was memorable because?"

"The Houdini-like trick was a record for the height of the dome and risk involved. I'm sure greater stunts have been staged but for Starfish Cove the dangle was huge."

The attendant called for boarding. There weren't many passengers and seats weren't assigned so we took the first ones, tucked our totes overhead and buckled our seatbelts.

Lizzy turned away from me fixing her gaze out the window.

"If you want to talk about your father, I'm here for you. If you want silence, I understand."

The passengers shuffled past, most carrying briefcases or laptop bags. The business of America rolled on. Everyday living was hard to comprehend when overwhelmed by personal tragedy. What was going through Lizzy's mind? I lost my father when I was a teenager. That cold ache flooded my heart anew. Because of her relationship with her father, her pain had to be different but no less devastating.

The attendant closed the door with a whomp! The plane engines began to wind. We taxied. The engines roared and we lifted off. "Our flying weather today is perfect," the pilot announced. "Sit back and enjoy the flight. We land in forty-five minutes."

I leaned toward Lizzy. "Why did Grams tell you about this Masked Dangler and why such a secret?"

"A combination of things but the shooting sealed the deal."

"Shooting? You mean people were getting murdered in Starfish Cove before I arrived?"

"Not a murder but an attempt. Grams said at this, his final performance, while the masked magician dangled high, arms spread, entrancing the crowd, two loud gunshots broke the silence."

She fiddled with a strand of hair, twisting it into a curl and then letting go. Hair fussing was her substitute for smoking.

"After the immediate shock of the noise wore off, some of the audience laughed. They thought it was part of the act."

She blew out a puff of air. "But the Dangler was bleeding. The arena crew quickly lowered him to the ground. People started running, stampeding over each other to get out of the place."

"You said attempted murder. What happened to him?"

"He lived but the story haunted me. Other magicians hated the Masked Dangler. He exposed the secrets behind their tricks and hurt their careers. The police and the hospital kept his identity hush-hush for his safety."

"But now someone is challenging him to a showdown? He must be kind of long in the tooth to execute high wire stunts. Why would he care if his identity were disclosed now? He's probably a harmless old man—maybe doesn't even live in the area."

"The Masked Dangler's not harmless. He's an egomaniac who retired holding the record for arena-dangling. It's the one award he dare not brag about."

"How do you know that?"

Lizzy looked at me without answering then lowered her head. She continued to stare at her knees. "This is the secret part of what Grams told me. My father was that masked magician."

Dingler was the Dangler!

CHAPTER 4

*T*he flight was as smooth as the pilot promised and we landed without incident. We went straight from the plane through the terminal to the parking lot.

Lizzy's VW bug, affectionately named Squeak—as in Bubble and Squeak—sat in the slot where we left it. We tossed our totes into the backseat.

She handed me the keys. "You drive. "I'm not up to it."

I wanted to say, "Drive this round-fendered thing that I can't possibly judge where the bumpers are?" Instead, I said, "No problem." I cheered myself with internal talk about the easy drive to sleepy Starfish Cove where a traffic jam was as rare as steak tartar. No problem was probably an accurate response. My fingers were crossed.

The trip went as smoothly as the flight until we reached the Old Town section of Starfish Cove. Ahead on the right was Nelson Dingler's six-story office building built when Old Town was new.

Lady Fortune continued to smile on me as I spotted a vacant parking space in front of the entrance. We'd be up in Dingler's apartment in a jiffy. Fortune's smile turned to a snarl when I realized the space was not a pull-in space. I had to parallel park.

Curbside parking was *not* one of my many talents—let alone in a car I never drove before. I glanced at Lizzy who hadn't spoken a word since we left the airport. She stared vacantly at the dashboard. I wasn't sure she even knew we'd arrived. I couldn't ask her to park the bubble-like car. I pushed my sunglasses to the top of my head—the better to see the darn curb.

I stopped next to the car in front of the vacant space, put it in reverse, and looked in the rearview mirror. I already had a line of three cars waiting for me to get out of the way. Where did they all come from? Did they lurk in alleys hoping for a good laugh at a non-parallel parker's expense?

The right rear wheel bumped the curb. I was in. I was about to congratulate myself on a job well done when I saw a third of the bug was still blocking the traffic lane and the line of waiting cars had doubled to six. A couple of drivers tooted their horns. Darn. I'd cut the wheels too sharply.

I turned the wheel to the right, pulled forward, stopped beside the car in front of the parking space, and repeated the backing up routine. This time I ended up perpendicular to the curb with half of the VW blocking the traffic lane. The line of waiting cars extended nearly to the cross street. More horns blew.

Was there a carnival in town, or a shell collectors' convention? The cars were multiplying faster than bunnies in spring.

A couple jogging on the sidewalk behind me stopped. The male jogger said, "Pull out again. I'll direct you in."

Sweat soaked through my bangs. I brushed them aside. Utter humiliation. I'm from New York City. We don't parallel park in the City. We have parking garages and valets—worth every penny.

The female jogger got in front of the bug and held out her hands when she thought I'd gone far enough. I started backing up and looked in the rearview mirror. The male jogger behind me gave a signal by turning his hand in a circle. But what did he mean? A mirror reverses images. Should I turn the wheel the way his hand was circling or the opposite way?

When I finished, the VW was again perpendicular to the curb. The line waiting now extended past the cross street, blocking the intersection. Horns started blaring from the cars at the intersection too. I pulled my sunglasses from the top of my head and covered my eyes hoping no one would recognize me.

The male jogger trotted up to the female jogger in front of me and said, "This is all your fault. You stopped her too soon."

"My fault?" she said. "You gave her bad directions and the only reason you stopped anyway is because she's pretty."

"The fact that she's pretty had nothing to do with it. I just wanted—"

"See you admit you noticed she's pretty." She pulled her belly pack from her waist

and started whapping him with it.

If they didn't get some emergency family therapy they might add to the Starfish Cove body count.

A heavy-duty woman charged off the sidewalk and thumped the male jogger in the shoulder. "You're not going to abuse this woman while I'm around."

The female jogger whapped her with the belly pack. "Leave my man alone!"

A guy the size of a rhino came out from between two parked cars and reached for the belly pack.

The male jogger stepped forward. "Get away from her."

The blaring horns got so loud I could no longer hear the combatants, but I could see them jawing at each other, blocking my path. Please let me drive away. I didn't care how far away the next parking spot might be.

I tooted my horn twice. The quarrelsome crew stepped onto the curb their mouths still yapping. I looked over my shoulder, signaled to pull out, and slid the VW between the nearest cars as if it were a greased pig.

Five parked cars down I saw a space. I sensed the collective groan from the drivers behind me. I had one shot to get it right. The VW cooperated fitting itself effortlessly into the spot. Okay, it was a space large enough for a tourist bus but still a minor miracle. I patted the dashboard as I shut off the engine. "Nice job, Squeak."

Once the parade of unreasonably irate drivers passed by, I popped out and ran around to the passenger side, opened the door, and shook Lizzy's shoulder to get her out of her trance. She looked up and said, "We're here already?"

"Yeah, it was a piece of cake."

CHAPTER 5

*M*y heart became heavy as I followed Lizzy into the building. Her father leased out the first two floors to the Pocket Change Bank. The next three floors were mostly single-practice lawyers' offices and a group of gynecologists. Nelson's apartment took up the entire sixth floor with his private rose garden on the roof.

Lizzy pushed the button marked Penthouse.

A few months earlier Dingler received a jolt to his ego. With the help of some men in weird T-shirts, Irma—wife number four—ran off taking with her all his furnishings including his treasured original painting by Frederick Remington. All accomplished while he was playing golf—Dingler, not Remington.

The haul amounted to a sizable take, especially for a brief marriage. Rumor was the furnishings became Irma's down payment for membership in a religious cult. According to Grams —also the source of the rumor—the members believed they were cosmically connected to a sister planet in one of the astrological constellations.

Probably no more absurd than Puff immersing herself in physics.

The elevator lurched to a halt on the sixth floor.

A crime scene tape decorated the cream-colored door of Nelson Dingler's residence. Lizzy knocked twice, then we stepped hesitantly into the huge living room—dining room combination with its polished stone floor. Gold was the dominant color. The overall effect was a honey-amber glow.

More of the yellow crime scene tape streamed about as if the room had been toilet papered. Fingerprint powder dusted the floor, the furnishings, and even drifted down from the high vaulted ceiling. The forensic team must have run amuck.

Kal stuck his head out the open doors directly across. "Here in the kitchen!"

We walked into a room that reflected Dingler's inner self. Plain white counters and matching enameled cabinets, not a wall decoration or personal touch in sight. Also no coffeemaker, toaster, juicer, or other usual small appliance. Irma must have run off with everything that wasn't bolted down.

Grams sat at a square four-person table. The tiny birdlike lady appeared half her normal size. She wore a bright pink retro dress, with a string of pastel beads around her neck and no gloves. She dabbed at her red swollen eyes with shaky hands. When she saw Lizzy she struggled to get up, catching her foot on the chair leg.

Kal caught Grams before she fell. He passed her to Lizzy's embrace and both women broke into tears. After a bit of sobbing, a lot less than Peroni-style mourning, we all took seats around the table. Kal's part-time assistant Robbie set a glass of water in front of Grams then stood in the corner watching us—concern on his young face.

Death's aura draped itself over me. A chill inched up my spine.

Grams bobbed her head at Kal and said in a choked voice, "Please tell the girls what happened."

He cast a kindly look at Grams before turning his attention to Lizzy. "We're here rather than the station because your grandmother has been through enough." He paused. "Your father is in the medical examiner's care."

A nicer way of saying he's on a slab in the morgue. I trampled over his considerate words. "You said something on the phone that didn't make sense—the cause of death was unnaturally natural?"

Lizzy pulled her chair close to Grams and put her arm around her.

"Grams found him hanging by his feet from the chandelier in the dining room."

"Let me tell it!" Grams said, giving her nose a short blow with a soggy tissue. "You're takin' too long."

She struggled from Lizzy's grip and refolded her miniature hands on the table. "I was working with Ivy at your cold cream shop when I got a call from that busybody assistant of Dr. Hudson's—the one who saw those cult nuts helping Irma carry off all of Nelson's things."

Grams took a deep breath and continued. "She said there was a heck of a racket coming from his apartment. Sounded like an argument. I called Nelson. He didn't answer his cellphone. He wasn't at the Yacht Club and they said his boat was in the marina. I hightailed it down here to check on him. No matter how old your child is, he's still your child."

She took a sip of water and cleared her throat. "I have a key for emergencies—never thought I'd live to use it. I opened the door and found my son hanging from the dining room chandelier by his feet. Someone had tied his ankles and hung him upside down like a dead goose."

Lizzy handed Grams a fresh tissue. She took it and pressed it to her nose.

19

"My son was no angel. Matter of fact he was a beast, but even a beast didn't deserve this. His face was blue." She let out a long sigh. "I tried to lift him a bit, so maybe he could breathe. I didn't have the strength but I knew when I touched him that he was gone." She let out a long sigh.

"Grams called me," Kal said. "Robbie and I arrived within minutes. But Mr. Dingler had indeed passed. The M.E.'s initial diagnosis is a stroke caused by the blood rushing to his head."

"Unnaturally natural," I said.

Pieces came into focus like one of those dot pictures that you have to stare at to see. I held my tongue not wanting to betray Lizzy's confidence. Nelson Dingler dangled to death. But why would he hang his old portly carcass by his ankles in his dining room? Practicing his trick to answer the challenge?

Kal said something, but the hamsters in the wheel of my mind were racing and his words failed to register. Did Nelson Dingler's death have anything to do with the ad in the *Silverfish Gazette*? He didn't tie his own ankles together, lasso the chandelier, and then hoist himself up twenty feet—or did he?

"Did anyone in the building see anything?" I asked. "It would take muscle or magic to lift him that high."

"Nobody saw or heard anything," Kal said. "That's why I need to know if you have any ideas, Lizzy. I'd ask you if your father had any enemies but…"

"Do ducks quack?" Lizzy said. "Sorry Grams."

Grams put her hand over Lizzy's. "It's okay sweetie. There's nothing you can tell me about your father that I don't already know."

As much as I wanted to ask about the magician's challenge in the *Silverfish Gazette*, my lips were sealed by my promise to Lizzy.

But Kal needed to know in order to catch the killer. How could I steer him in the right direction without betraying Lizzy and Gram's secret?

CHAPTER 6

*L*izzy sat with her arm around Grams, neither crying but their eyes were moist. I stepped behind them, scooched down, and put my hands on their shoulders "I'm so sorry."

I kissed Grams on the cheek. "If there is anything I can do." Cliché but timeless. I couldn't bring Nelson back, but I *could* help find his killer.

Standing up, I beckoned Kal to follow me. Lizzy and Grams were lost in their silence. We slipped out of the kitchen. I said, "As your unpaid, unofficial investigator and criminal profiler can I inspect the crime scene?"

He hesitated and shrugged. "Your thoughts about the scene are where your involvement stops. Dingler was a big deal in this town and I don't need you amping up the media."

Hmmm, was he a little testy because of the *Silverfish Gazette* coverage of the last Starfish Cove homicide? That was months ago. He should have recovered by now.

He led me through the apartment. We left a trail of footprints through the fine fingerprint powder. The stuff was everywhere.

I fought back a sneeze. Even the Magoo brothers—Starfish Cove's befuddled forensic team—weren't this sloppy.

When we reached the open-plan dining room, I noticed a tall ladder marked *Starfish Cove PD* standing against the wall but didn't comment on it. "What's with all the powder? The Magoos?"

"Yes. No. Sort of." Kal's face reddened. "I helped make the mess. Tim climbed their ladder to dust the chandelier while Tom went to their van to get a hand-vac they left behind. Tim forgot to take the powder up the ladder with him and asked me to toss it to him."

"You didn't!"

"I did. It was the largest container of the stuff I've ever seen. I forgot to check the screw-on lid before I pitched it. He didn't catch it cleanly. It smacked the top rung, the lid popped off just as the air conditioner kicked on and blew powder throughout the apartment."

I got the giggles. If he ever heard about my parallel parking traffic jam, I had a counterpunch.

"Hey! It's not that funny."

I got myself under control and said, "What's your theory?"

"You're here to tell me what you think, not vice versa."

"If you keep this up, I'm going to demand a twenty percent raise."

He smiled. "That would completely bust the budget so I'll give you the inside scoop. I don't have the foggiest idea what happened."

"That's your professional police evaluation?"

"More or less. Weirdest thing I've ever seen. Suicide's out unless he was really confused and put the rope around his feet instead of his neck—but then the button to raise and lower the chandelier for maintenance would have been out of his reach. It's inside the service closet."

"Surely not an accident," I said.

"Not unless you want to believe he was trying to reach the

chandelier without lowering it but he slipped and got tangled in his safety line. I can't picture Dingler trying to change a light bulb. Besides Grams already told me that he had a maintenance man take care of the place."

"You're leaning towards murder?"

"Murder seems as unlikely. Who would hang him from the chandelier instead of just choking him?"

"A chimpanzee with an attitude?"

Kal glared at me.

I poked my chin toward the ceiling. "Did the killer move the dining table out from under the light fixture to make room for Dingler to dangle?"

"If there is a killer—human or simian—he could have stood on it, but the scuffmarks indicate it was pushed out of the way. A deliberate dangle."

If Nelson were practicing for the magician's challenge, he'd probably be in tights—if they made tights that big. "What was Dingler wearing?"

"Khaki trousers, a white shirt, dress shoes and socks. No watch, no jewelry. It might be robbery and murder."

"But like you pointed out, why bother stringing him up?" Leading Kal in the right direction without giving away Dingler's secret wasn't easy. "Maybe the killer was making a statement."

Kal shook his head. "Dingler could drive a saint to pull off this stunt. He was a bombastic bully but nobody deserves to go like this."

"Maybe the killer didn't intend for him to die. Where's the rope? We might learn something from the way the knot was tied."

"What do you mean by we? You are *not* invited."

"Need I remind you of my success rate, not to mention my potential request for a salary increase?"

"Lizzy and WonderDog helped you make headlines. You might

want to enlist the help of your kitten this time. This is a case for a climber—Puff the magic kitten."

I ignored his crack about not being invited and charged on. "Did the Magoos take the evidence back to the station?"

"Not Magoo. McCool. They had a coughing fit from the powder and left without their equipment and evidence bag. It's over there by the door."

I scurried over, grabbed the satchel and dragged it back to Kal. "Isn't it time Starfish Cove got themselves a competent forensic team? The Magoos are a disaster."

"As long as their uncle is State Attorney, we're stuck with them. The county CSI sticks them in the Cove to keep them out of the way."

I stooped over the bag. "Got a pair of latex gloves?"

"Here." He handed me blue vinyl gloves from his trouser pocket. I held them while I continued to study the heavy cord.

"Flashlight?" Even in the shadow of the bag, the rope had sheen to it. Those Magoos would miss an elephant in the room.

Kal's small light cast a bright beam into the evidence sack. I touched the tip of my bare index finger to one spot on the rope. Slimy.

"Don't! Not without gloves," Kal barked.

I rubbed my thumb against the slippery gunk on my finger and held it out to him.

"What?" He looked annoyed, but curious.

"It's soap. There's soap on this rope!"

He rubbed my finger. This was hardly the time for the warm reaction I had. I pulled my hand away and said too sharply, "Soap. No doubt in my mind, soap."

Kal squinted as he moved his gaze from my finger to my eyes.

The only thing that stopped me from telling him everything right then was that I'd given my word to keep the secret about Dingler the Masked Dangler. The soap- coated rope guaranteed that if Dingler found the strength to haul himself up, he'd lose his grip.

This was no practice-related accident.

Before I could spill the beans or at least open the can, Lizzy tottered into the room with Grams leaning on her. She turned her back shielding her grandmother from the black evidence bag. She spoke over her shoulder. "I convinced Grams to spend the night at my place. We're going to her house to pick up a nightie and her medicine. Olive can you drive us?"

Grams looked like a fragile pastry about to crumble.

"Sure." I flipped the evidence bag closed while my stomach tightened at the thought of driving Squeak. "Who's watching Heather right now?" I was ashamed that I hadn't thought about Lizzy's ward earlier.

"She went home from school with one of her little friends. Three teachers' work days this week and then the weekend. She loves sleepovers. Has anyone called my sister?" Lizzy looked from Grams to Kal.

"Sorry," Kal said. "I thought it better if you tell Pam."

"I'll call her at the hospital when we get to Grams' house. She's been working long shifts because of the nursing shortage." Lizzy's eyes watered.

"Meet you and Grams at the elevator," I said.

Once they were gone I whispered, "Don't let the Magoos have this rope." I zipped the bag and pushed it in his direction. "I'm driving Lizzy's VW. My car is at my condo. Can you pick me up at her house in about an hour?"

"Of course. I want to hear more about the soap on this rope before we have it evaluated."

"Not by the Magoos!"

I hoped I didn't sound as freaked as I felt.

Those guys could screw up an anvil.

CHAPTER 7

Grams' cottage sat in the heart of the residential section of Old Town. The homes in her neighborhood were mostly bungalows, small in size but big in character. No two were alike but all had a sweet charm about them.

Dusk settled over the peaceful community as we rolled down the street in the VW until Grams' white lap-siding bungalow came into view. The indoor and outdoor lights were on—probably a timer. The place looked cute, aged, and inviting just like its owner.

I drove around the white picket fence, pulled into the short brick driveway, and shut off the engine.

The seating in the VW was tight. Grams took my hand as I helped her out. She'd aged ten years—no wonder.

Lizzy squeezed out of the back seat—first one wedgie then the other. The aroma of WonderDog trailed her. Sitting in the hound's rear navigator post had left its mark.

I grabbed my tote from the back, hoping the mark of WonderDog hadn't spread to the other side.

Lizzy and I held Grams as she shuffled up the brick walkway leading to the front porch. With a hand on the wrought iron railing I braced my other hand around her back in case she slipped from Lizzy's grip.

"The pansies need watering," Grams said.

A lovely flowerbed of purple pansies bordered the stairs. The landscaping was as whimsical as its owner. A whiff of wild flowers and gardenia lent a calming air to the adrenalin thrumming through my body.

"I'll take care of the pansies later," Lizzy said. She took the key from her grandmother and opened the door.

I'd been in Grams' cottage before, but the charm of the place struck me anew with its gleaming oak hardwood floors, a small fireplace of rough white stone, tiny arched doorways, crown molding, and plantation shutters—all it needed was Goldilocks.

"I'll help get your suitcase out in a minute." Lizzy walked her grandmother to her bedroom and then pulled me aside. "I have to phone my sister and tell her. I don't think I should do it in front of Grams. Can you help her while make the call?"

"Sure. How are you doing?"

"I'm over the initial shock. It is what it is," she said in a monotone voice. "My father's dead."

She stepped into the sunroom pulling a phone from the pocket of her jumpsuit.

Grams sat on a single bed with a quilt of pink, blue, and white. She rubbed the heel of her hand against her chest.

"Are you in pain?" I asked.

"Just thinking." She wiped at her nose. "I have an idea who did this to Nelson. I'm going to see that he pays for it. My son must have suffered horribly."

This was one of those times when a lie was necessary. "The medical examiner told Kal it was painless. A stroke can be that way. Quick."

She ignored my words of consolation. "We're gonna get him, Olive," she pounded one fist into the other. "You, me, and Lizzy!"

The little lady stood up, dropped to her knees and pulled a small overnight bag from under the bed. She moved quickly, like a woman one-third her age, determination suddenly fueling her.

She bagged a pair of pink slippers and tucked them in the case. She took a nightie from a drawer and laid it on top. Then she hurried into the bathroom. In a twinkling she returned with a toothbrush and paste in a clear plastic bag. A second bag held a hairbrush and a jar of Nonna's cold cream.

"You and Lizzy are close. I'm guessing she told you about Nelson."

A knot formed in my throat. I closed my eyes for a long moment hoping Grams wouldn't ask me what I knew. She didn't ask. She shared the secret with me. I felt like one of the family.

"Pinky promise, tell no one!" Her eyes turned steely.

I nodded. How could someone so tiny be so scary?

"Nelson was the Masked Dangler. He hung from great heights by his feet—broke all sorts of national dangling records. By the time he was twenty he was a legend in Starfish Cove even though his identity was a secret. But that boy had a mean streak. The more successful he got the meaner he turned. The local magicians hated him." She slowly shook her head.

"He began to expose the illusions behind other magician's tricks. My son ruined a lot of magical careers. Whoever killed him came from the Magicians' League. It has all the marks of a professional trick."

I didn't want to disagree but if the killer was a magician, he or she was the dumbest prestidigitator in Florida. The ad in *The Silverfish Gazette* was like a neon sign pointing right at the perpetrator.

"Somebody calling himself the Phantom challenged the Masked Dangler with an ad in the *Gazette*. Shouldn't be too hard to find out who paid for that ad."

She snapped her suitcase shut. "We're going to find the killer before this highly hyped Magician's Fusion. It's set for April Fools' Day—two weeks from today. Darned if I'm going to wait on the police. The less they know about Nelson's secret past the better. I'll continue to say it was a robbery gone real bad, but it wasn't. It was revenge."

Lizzy stepped into the room. "Pam's coming from Jacksonville tomorrow. She thinks we should leave it up to the police."

Grams threw back her boney shoulders. "We're not going to rely on the cops. You, me, and Olive are going to catch Nelson's killer. Pam can join us if she wants. Nurses always come in handy."

She stepped to the closet and rummaged in a pile of folded sweaters.

Lizzy covered her mouth with her hand and whispered. "Pam doesn't know about the Masked Dangler. We never told her. I wonder how she's going to take it?"

Grams tottered towards us slipping her arms into a light pink sweater. "I'm ready. Let's boogie."

While Lizzy helped Grams secure her house for the night, I stepped out on the porch. Standing in the wraparound corner, I tapped Ivy LaVine's number on speed dial. We'd only been gone since the morning and yet it felt like I'd abandoned our cold cream shop.

Ten years younger than Grams, it took Ivy eleven rings to answer. I made allowances for her age while patiently counting the jingles. I imagined her dozing in front of her television while watching *Murder She Wrote* on an oldies cable channel.

"Ivy here!" Her voice sounded like someone crushing tissue paper.

"Sorry to bother you. How did it go at the shop?"

"Not bad. We had a bunch of customers right after Mrs. Dingler got a call from her son's neighbor. When she couldn't reach him she panicked. Have you heard from her? Is she okay?"

"We're with her right now." I hoped Ivy didn't ask about

Nelson. Gossip traveled faster than Superman on roller skates in Starfish Cove.

"Is Nelson Dingler okay?" she asked.

Nuts! I struggled for a way to avoid answering. Nothing came to me—so I put my foot in my mouth. "He met with an accident."

"How bad?"

"Dead bad. But don't tell anyone."

One single gasp later Myron Meyers—my former patient and a retired maybe-crime boss took over the phone. "What's this I'm hearing? Sweet Lizzy's father bit the big one?"

The octogenarian's use of the English language was a work of art—graffiti.

"Are you cohabitating with Ivy? You're always at her place."

Breathless voices were followed by the thud of what sounded like a headboard hitting a wall. They'd been canoodling.

"Nose out of my personal business," Myron said. "What's going on? Did he take a bullet? 'Ya need help?"

"The Medical Examiner called it natural. Put Ivy back on —please."

There was a bit of shuffling, a groan or two, and Ivy returned.

"Do what you have to do to help Mrs. Dingler," she said. "If you need me tomorrow I can shop-sit again. I locked up tight as a...as a...well you know." Failing to find the word she rolled along. "I left a note on the counter with a list of suggestions. I can't wait to hear about your visit with Sophia Napoli."

"I promise to tell you all about it in the next few days." I clicked off.

"Everything okay at the shop?" Lizzy asked. She stepped out on the porch holding the door for her grandmother with one hand and the overnight bag with the other.

"It's all good. No problems."

Grams watched from the porch as Lizzy wedgied down the stairs.

SOAP ON A ROPE

Lizzy reached over the flowerbed and turned on the hose. Still in a fog, she gave the pansies a quick sprinkle, hit the gardenia bush with a spray, and watered the porch steps.

"Let's get going, girls." Grams tugged on a pair of pink crocheted gloves and bent to pick up her bag.

Lizzy scrambled up the dripping stairs, took the overnight bag from her grandmother, and said, "I'm still not up to driving," giving me her one-eyebrow pleading look.

"I'll take you home. Squeak is actually fun to drive if you like maneuvering a handle-less teacup in traffic."

My friend clambered into the backseat holding Grams' bag. I handed her my tote and guided Grams into place.

When I started to buckle her seat belt she smacked my hand. "Don't you dare! I'm not a child."

Chastened, I ran around the car and slipped behind the steering wheel. Squeak chirped into action. I eased down the driveway checking the cottage in the rearview mirror. Grams' house looked occupied with lights on and water dripping from the steps. It would be safe for the night.

Anyone watching Squeak cruise down the street would never guess the car carried three determined killer-magician hunters.

CHAPTER 8

*K*al wasn't waiting for me at Lizzy's. Too bad. I wanted to be sure the women were safe inside for the night. What if the entire Dingler family was in danger? I reached inside my tote feeling around for my can of self-defense hair spray. Unarmed! Not allowed on the flight, I'd left it home.

A slobbering red tongue greeted Lizzy as she unlocked her door. "Enough WonderDog! Sit!"

Instead of obeying, the gangly hound pawed at the front door once Lizzy closed it.

"Dave was supposed to walk WonderDog before the dinner rush. I don't think he's been emptied. Maybe Dave couldn't break away."

She clipped a leash to the dog that bore a striking resemblance to the wolf in *Little Red Riding Hood*. "Be right back."

"Grams would you like some tea? Maybe Lizzy has some chamomile?"

"That would be nice dear."

We left her bag at the door and walked into the kitchen.

A bright turquoise teakettle sat on the stove. I filled it with water, but hesitated. One of Lizzy's new finches swooped down and landed on my shoulder. Fearful that turning on the gas stove might result in an injury to the bird, I stopped my tea making.

Two minutes later, Lizzy returned. She unleashed WonderDog who leaped on me dripping kisses. Despite his doggy breath I could never resist him.

"I was going to make tea, but I don't want to hurt the finches. How do you turn on the stove without the finches getting burned?"

"Easy peasy." She took a stick of incense from a drawer and placed it in a holder on the stove. The kitchen birds beat a retreat to the other rooms as if a hawk perched on the refrigerator.

Grams and I exchanged eye-rolls.

"Why did you replace your seventy-six lost finches with fifty-two?" I asked.

"Because the pet store didn't have seventy-six, they only had fifty-two. Fifty is a sensible number but I couldn't leave two behind. That would be cruel." She turned on the burner.

The sound of Grams' soft chuckle was followed by a knock on the door.

"Come in!" Lizzy called.

I made a mental note to warn her about not locking the door and being so free to invite knockers.

Kal stepped into a WonderDog greeting complete with a sticky, smelly tongue—the dog's not Kal's.

"Everything okay here?" He gave the combination family room and kitchen a quick scan.

Grams shot a button-your-lip look at Lizzy and me. She'd dug in her pink orthopedic heels—determined to catch her son's killer without Kal's help.

"I won't rest until the mystery of Nelson's death is solved," Kal said.

Grams didn't respond. She plucked a *Sweet Dreams* tea bag from the jar on the counter, dropped it into a cup and poured boiling water over it. She'd written Kal out of her investigation.

The officer smiled at the Dingler ladies and then turned to me. "Ready, Olive?"

I hugged Lizzy and approached Grams but she was in the process of balancing a hot cup on a saucer. "See you tomorrow." She pointedly addressed me, excluding Kal.

Lizzy walked us to the door.

"Lock this tight. Windows, too!" I said.

She squinted her eyes until they were two amber slits. "You're thinking Grams and I are in danger? I'll have Dave spend the night."

"How are you fixed for hairspray?" Neither one of us could bring ourselves to use pepper spray—too cruel.

"I've got a can by each door. We'll be fine." WonderDog trotted to her side ready to protect her.

Kal and I were silent walking to his police car. He held the passenger door open, pressed my head with his hand, and pushed me into the seat.

"Am I under arrest?"

He reddened. "Sorry about that. Force of habit."

I snorted. Despite the pine-scented tree that dangled from the mirror, the car smelled of criminals.

"What do you think?" He said, turning on the engine. "About Dingler?"

I was really in a spot. I should tell him what I knew or guessed. But a secret is a secret. A pledge is a pledge.

"Too strange for me to have a reliable opinion yet. Do you have the rope with you?"

"I'm taking it over to the county lab for analysis. Chandelier dangling from a soapy rope isn't something that comes up in any criminology classes."

We drove in silence to Sandy Shores Towers. There were times when things became too comfortable between Kal and me. It was nice to have him stop in occasionally to talk crime solving, but I wasn't looking for a relationship. My life revolved around *Nonna's Cold Cream* shop—affairs of the heart could wait.

Kal pulled into the parking lot under the building. He shut off the motor. After an awkward silence peppered with deep breaths and intense stares at the moonlit Gulf waters, Kal spoke. "Can we continue this conversation upstairs?"

If there was a conversation in play I wasn't hearing it but I welcomed the chance to pick his brains... and that was the only reason to spend more time with him.

"Puff's probably worried by now." I pushed on the handle eager to escape the vibe he sent out.

Stepping quickly around the car Kal opened my door. I held my noggin with both hands protecting it from any further head grabbing.

He laughed and raised his hands in the universal gesture of surrender.

We hurried up the steps and down the walkway to my condo. Was it only this morning that I leaped into Lizzy's VW bursting with anticipation over meeting Sophia Napoli?

I fumbled through my purse for the key, slipped it in the lock, and opened the door.

Kal moved past me, his flashlight dancing over the foyer and then into the kitchen on the right and the living room on the left.

His *Miami Vice* entrance into my darkened condo grated on me. I would have mocked him but I'd had a prowler once. Better annoyed, then mugged.

I clicked on the lights.

Curled in a ball on the sofa, Puff stretched and yawned. She jumped down, trotted to me, and surrounded my legs with love and fuzz. I bent to pet her, rubbing under her chin—a favorite spot.

"Take a seat in the kitchen. I'll put on coffee."

Once I'd filled our mugs and set out the cream, I sat across from Kal wondering what rules he was going to lay down and which ones I would ignore.

He held Puff against his chest. As a reward she shed her trademark white fur on his black Starfish Cove Police shirt. If this case dragged on I'd gift him with a box of lint rollers.

He locked eyes with me. "Don't try to solve Nelson's death on your own. It makes no sense so I can't say if it's murder. However if it is, the method screams maniac. Lizzy and Grams and even Pam may be in jeopardy. For their sakes tell me what you know."

He had me trapped! I chewed on my lip.

Kal's eyes lasered me. He didn't relent even when Puff climbed up his chest her claws tugging his polo shirt. I could swear she was trying to distract him but he wasn't going for it.

"I pinky-promised Lizzy and Grams…" It was Grams' term for a binding promise.

"So is there some dark Dingler secret?"

"I'll be right back."

The *Silverfish Gazette* came out whenever news, coupons, or events like our Cold Cream Shop Open House demanded it. My souvenir issue with the photo of Lizzy and me lay on the desk in my little home office. The headline above the fold proclaimed *Murder at the Marina* with the ad challenging the Masked Dangler on the flip side.

Returning to the kitchen I placed the newspaper on the table so the challenge lay face up.

Kal glanced at it. "Does this publicity stunt have something to do with Nelson Dingler's death?"

"I'd offer you another cup but I really need to get to sleep." I dodged his question.

He pushed the newspaper aside, stood, and handed me Puff.

There was still coffee in his cup but he ignored it—maybe because a cat hair floated on top.

We walked to the door. The mewing kitten wiggled in my arms trying to reach Kal. He stroked her head, offered me a terse good night, and left.

I gave him a clue without breaking my promise. It was up to him to figure it out.

CHAPTER 9

*P*uff purred in my ear and then head-butted my cheek. I opened one eye. The early morning sun was melting the night sky. The comforting sound of the waves lapping on the shore accompanied by the cries of the gulls announced all was right with the world—aside from Nelson Dingler resting on a pullout slab in the M.E.'s refrigerator.

The phone jangled Lizzy's ringtone. "I just took Grams to get her car. She left it parked on the street in front of my father's office. I'll be in the shop by nine."

Great. A nonagenarian parallel-parked an ancient aircraft carrier-sized car. My ego whispered ouch. Grams' Edsel was the last one off the production line back in 1960—the vehicle flopped because it was so huge—exactly why Grams treasured it.

"How are you? How's Grams?"

"As well as can be expected. She's headed to the *Starfish Gazette* hole-in-the-wall office to pull up the invoice for that ad. I begged her not to chase after any killers without us."

"Definitely! We'll go with her to track down the challenger after we close the shop. She's too old to go it alone."

"Don't use the 'o' word around her. Being called *old* gets Grams steamed up. Finding the person who murdered my father has put a spring in her step. She's determined to get the guy." Lizzy paused. "You didn't tell Kal about the Dangler?"

"Not a word." Just a clue.

"Grams screeched the tires and squealed off in her Edsel. It won't take her long to come up with something about that ad. She has me believing whoever placed it wanted to draw the Dangler out to kill him."

"I hope it's as simple as that."

"We have reinforcements coming in. My sister Pam will be in town this afternoon."

Puff stared at me sending a telepathic message—I'm hungry.

"I have a starving cat sending me on a guilt trip. See you at the shop." I rolled out of bed with a kitty at my feet.

While Puff gobbled down a can of chicken paté, I fired up the coffeemaker. A few minutes later I sat on the balcony sipping while staring at the blue-gray waters of the Gulf of Mexico. The barely perceptible voices of shell seekers walking along the beach competed with squawking gulls disturbing my peace as I ruminated about the case.

A gull swooped in and landed on the rail. He tilted his head inspecting my coffee cup. No cookies. No crackers. No chunks of bread. Lifting his beak in what looked like a snub, he left me a splat, flapped his wings, and flew off.

This was not going to be a good day.

I pulled on black jersey slacks and a matching top. My black ballet flats weren't the best for standing on my feet all day but I slipped them on without much thought. Might need the magician's ad—I stuffed the *Silverfish Gazette* in my tote.

Puff lounged on the sofa waiting for her goodbye kiss. I touched my lips to her forehead loving the baby-like smell of her soft fur. She licked my hand and we parted for the day.

Lizzy was already at the shop when I got there. She wore a zippered black jumpsuit with a simple locket on a gold chain. Her curls were swept back in a barrette. A believable smile graced her face. She'd overcome the initial shock.

Gathering plastic balls of lip gloss Lizzy placed them one by one in a wicker display basket. Getting back into our shop routine would be good for both of us.

I leaned on the counter opposite her. "You okay?"

"It's all going to work out. We'll find my father's killer and he can rest in peace. I had a long talk with myself last night. I have to accept I never won his approval but perhaps he'll learn some lessons about unconditional love in the afterlife."

She chuckled softly. "I had a dream he was standing at an old-fashioned blackboard writing *I will be kind to my daughters* over and over again, while a nun whapped him on the butt with a ruler."

"Sounds like a terrific dream to me."

After nesting the last few ball-shaped lip gloss containers into a pink wicker basket, she reached under the counter and pulled out a tablet. The top page had numbered paragraphs on it. She studied it for a few seconds then pushed it to me. "Look at this."

It was written in a delicate hand.

"Ivy mentioned leaving a note, she failed to mention it was three pages long." I said as I picked up the tablet and began to read aloud.

"Dear Olive and Lizzy,

Thank you for letting me shop-sit. It's been so much fun. I hope you don't mind but I jotted down a few suggestions as I once worked at the cosmetic counter at Macy's in Manhattan—until they fired me but it wasn't my fault. Remind me to tell you about the lady with the rash. Anyway, I have years of valuable experience and since you girls are new to the business I can be an asset."

"Have a seat," Lizzy said. "I don't like the sound of that years of experience—or the rash."

I hooked my foot around the leg of a stool and slid it into place. Comparing the cosmetic counter at Macy's with Nonna's Cold Cream Shop was like equating a freight train with a bicycle. I continued to read aloud.

"Here are a few ideas that popped into my mind while I was meeting your darling customers. I'm having a few of them over for tea on Saturday. You're welcome to come. I can't wait to get cooking on these improvements—don't take offense but you gals need my help."

"Are you offended?" I asked Lizzy.

"Not yet but you're only on the first page." A smile played around the corners of her mouth.

"Number one. We need tons more free samples. I'd given away all that you had by lunchtime. People were so excited. They filled up their purses and beach bags. The big cosmetic companies give away lots of samples. That's how you hook ladies on your cream."

"Geez Louise!" I laid the tablet on the counter and wrung my face with my hands. "I don't even want to look. There were four cartons of samples in the back yesterday morning. We just spent two weeks of after-shop hours filling those tiny jars! Ivy gave them away in one day! One half day!"

"This one might have some merit." Lizzy picked up Ivy's instructions and read on.

"Number two. Have your customers return their empty jars for a dollar discount off a new jar of cream. I'm sure you're paying more than that for those fancy glass jars. We can sterilize them in your home dishwasher."

"Why do I find that yucky?" I scrunched my nose. "We'd be faced with a hefty fine from the health department."

"Seeing how you loathe colognes, you're going to love this one," Lizzy continued.

"How about a designer perfume? You could call it Olive &

Lizzy's Garden. I can help you with that. I have a renowned sense of smell."

I laid my head on the counter and covered it with my hands. Despite my position I was unable to muffle the giggles.

"Myron?" Lizzy said. It was a rhetorical question.

I lifted my head just enough to nod. "Ivy's sense of smell is more like a sinus condition. She's nuts about Myron and he smells like an old taxi cab."

I stopped laughing long enough to ask, "Do you get the feeling she's messing with our minds? What scares me most is her frequent use of the *we* word."

Lizzy gulped back a chuckle and read more this time mimicking Ivy's tissue paper voice.

"I got an idea from a nice young man who bought up our entire supply of lavender soap. He wanted it for wedding shower favors. Isn't that sweet? Let's think of making goodie bags for special events. Don't you *love* that idea?"

Lizzy put her hand on her chest as if enamored with the idea of goodie bags.

"I'm happy she sold them instead of giving them away. There were two boxes of twenty-four bars each in the back." I slid off the stool. "I need to stand to get the blood flowing to my brain."

"Listen to this," Lizzy said. "She's redesigning our packaging now." She lowered her voice as she read. "I think we should change the color of our packaging from pink to something more eye-catching like orange. Pink is too sissy which brings me to my next suggestion."

I groaned.

Lizzy waved her hand in a flourish toward the shop entrance. "We need a blinking sign at the road. Maybe in the shape of a cold cream jar but with an arrow pointing to the parking lot. The shop is hard to see if you're speeding down Starfish Boulevard."

"The speed limit is thirty-five miles per hour," I said.

"Later, two gents in business suits stopped in. They sniffed around but didn't stay long. I tried to chat them up but they weren't the talkative type."

I raised my eyebrows at Lizzy. She wiggled hers and returned to reading, this time making her voice sound husky.

"We need a line of beauty creams for men. This place is too feminine. Maybe we can pipe in musk? Consider serving beer besides tea. We could pour it in nice chilled mugs. Guys like that."

I laughed so hard tears dribbled down my cheeks. "Hand me that last page. I need to do the reading. You're hamming it up and making it twice as funny."

Lizzy handed it over.

I blotted my eyes and cleared my throat. Unable to stop myself, I read in my own version of Ivy's voice.

"It couldn't hurt to add two small tables by the windows. I measured. They'd fit. Ladies might like to have tea and cookies while they shop. Seated by the window customers would get a lovely view of the boulevard. I called the city to see what kind of permit you'd have to get. You need a food and beverage license. They're expensive but you can make up for it in sales."

"Oh no! Now the city thinks we want a café license!" I returned to reading aloud, feeling invisible fingers tighten around my throat. "You are almost out of cold cream. I rummaged in the backroom but couldn't find any more jars. Afraid I missed a couple of customers when I was back there. Didn't hear them come in but —sorry about this—they seem to have taken your standing mirrors from the counter. Tell me what they cost. I'll reimburse you."

I glanced at the counters. The three expensive, magnifying mirrors were missing. Lizzy shrugged as I went back to reading.

"I called Myron right way. He came by and stood security at the door. Sorry but he scared off a few customers pretending to have a gun in his jacket pocket. One lady asked if he was Michael Corleone! Myron is so adorable."

I slammed the tablet on the counter and hugged myself. "Why hadn't we thought about selling beer in chilled mugs? It's such an obvious tie-in or with every jar of cold cream you get a free beer."

Lizzy chuckled. "How about including spicy chicken wings? There's space for a deep fryer near the back door."

It took a long time for us to stop laughing.

"We've created a monster. Extracting Ivy from our business is going to be more painful than a do-it-yourself root canal."

I wiped the tears from my eyes as the bell over the door announced a visitor.

CHAPTER 10

"*P*oshookly!"

Jaimie Toast sashayed into the shop looking pretty, healthy, and almost sober.

Cancelling her divorce from Chip Toast continued to work wonders for the *Loud Mouth of the South*. Always attractive in a pushy way Chip's recent inheritance allowed Jaimie to frequent the best spas and most exclusive products. Our tolerance for her sarcasm and Nonna's cold cream always drew her back to our little circle.

I imagined the music from *Pretty Woman* setting her pace as she strode from the door to the counter. She dropped her designer bag on the glass with a clunk and grabbed Lizzy's hand.

"Never fear! Jaimie's here." Releasing Lizzy, she reached in her bag and pulled out a silver flask. "How about a screwdriver? Takes the edge off."

I hadn't seen her since she returned from four weeks at The Golden Aches Spa somewhere out west. She appeared ten pounds trimmer, her complexion radiant, and her hair silky. Too bay they weren't able to solve her snarkiness, which kicked in the moment she opened her bee-stung lips.

"Sorry to hear about old popurcusew!" She patted Lizzy's hand. "Driving over here I tried to think of some words of consolation but all I could conjure was—sure hope the frolog left you something in his will. If he left you his yacht I think I have a buyer for it!" She cocked her head. "Because you're a friend I'll only charge a ten-percent brokerage fee."

Lizzy pulled her hand from Jaimie's grip. "Poshookly! How can you think of money when my father is barely cold?"

Jaimie narrowed her eyes and her face turned crimson. "Poshookly is *my* word. I don't ever want to hear you saying it again. Got that?" She rolled her eyes back into her head searching. "I'll give you your own word—you can say crumb cakes! I'll give you that for free, but no poshookly!"

I scrunched my face for Lizzy's benefit. Where Jaimie was concerned it was easier to pretend to go along.

"Now back to old Nelson Dingler. How can you *not* think of money at a time like this? Your father owes you make-up money and I don't mean in a cosmetic way. He treated you shabby. When's the reading of his will? I'll go with you to be sure you get your share."

Jaimie Toast was all heart. No soul—just a heart—of stone.

She rummaged through the lip gloss display oblivious to the looks Lizzy and I exchanged. "Rumor is Nelson committed suicide, hung himself." She snuck a look at us gauging our reaction.

"They're investigating." Lizzy said. A knot appeared under her cheekbone as she clenched her jaw.

"So Miss Olive, you and your special friend, Officer Kal, tag-teaming this one?"

Jaimie could be amusing at times—this was not one of those times. I stepped behind the counter, tucked my tote underneath, and proceeded to cut her off. "Lizzy just lost her father. Have a little respect. Are you here to buy or to snark?"

She breezed past my dig. "Word on the street is you're out of lavender soap. I guess just a jar of your magical cream will do. By the way the director of the Golden Aches Spa wanted to know what I was using on my face. He thinks it's nothing short of a miracle."

She glanced up and down the counter top. "Hey! Where's your mirrors?"

Not about to tell her we'd been shoplifted, I said, "We sent them out for sanitizing." It was a fibberoo but she believed it.

"Makes sense." She leaned over the counter turning her face right and left to catch her reflection in the glass top. "I do look good. You should consider talking to this guy from the Golden Aches. He could put you on the map."

"Thanks, but we're on the map in Starfish Cove and for now that suits us!"

She plunked down a credit card, while Lizzy packaged her cold cream. "If it wasn't suicide and if—I'm just saying if—someone bumped off Nelson, I'd look at the sharks vying for his seat as Commodore of the Yacht Club. Need I remind you every robuggy who held that post has died in office? Just saying. Those who ignore history are bound to get killed—or something like that.'"

Robuggy? Alice in Wonderland would have envied Jaimie's vocabulary.

She took her pink package from Lizzy. "Chip and I are thinking of having a housewarming in April. Keep the month open cause we haven't picked the date yet." She grabbed her bag by the handles and wiggled her manicured fingers. "Toodle-loo! Don't do anything I wouldn't do."

That left the field wide open.

She swanned to the door bumping into Nancy Nemo who barged into the shop like a bull. The owner of Crabby Nancy's

Fried Fish didn't favor Jaimie with a greeting but then again, Nancy wasn't big on hellos, goodbyes, or anything in between.

Our new customer stomped to the counter. "I'm here for a jar of your cold cream. My face is cracking like an over-fried hush-puppy—must be from being out on my boat. Bound to get worse," she spoke in rapid fire. "I'm thinking of sailing to Nevis Island. Plan on being gone for six or eight months. Better give me two jars."

Nancy gave Lizzy a smirk. "Dave's going to have his hands full running the restaurant without me." She lowered her voice, looked to the right and then the left. "Anyone else here besides you two?"

"Just us." Nancy had confided in me in the past. Though considerably older she brought out my maternal instincts. She could do with psychological sessions and a facial, but I wasn't about to volunteer for either. The sailing restaurateur could be bull-headed and scary at times.

"I heard about Nelson Dingler," she whispered. "Peculiar way to knock somebody off."

Obviously Nancy's rumor was more accurate than Jaimie's. I said, "Any rumors about who did it?"

She shook her head. "More worms in this killing than a bait box. But I'll leave it up to you gals—seeing how you're the ones with the Sherlock Holmes reputations. One piece of advice—keep in mind the turnover of Yacht Club Commodores is like flipping fishcakes—fast and furious." She laughed but then converted her chuckle into a cough.

"Sorry Lizzy. I wasn't laughing about your father." She leaned in so close her nose almost touched mine. "There's one guy you need to keep an eye on. Rex Marchmain. He hired a bodyguard last week and kicked off his campaign this morning. He's looking to replace Dingler as Commodore."

Hmmm. Two rumormongers back-to-back tying it to the

commodoreship. Maybe it was worth considering. "Was March-main buddies with Nelson? There was no sign of forced entry."

Nancy snorted. "Lizzy grew up around these would-be Commodores. Did you ever see any two of them get along? Buddies? Hah!"

"They're like feral fish," Lizzy said. "They'd devour each other if given a chance."

"Exactly. No love lost. But keep an eye on Rex as I won't be here to help you. I saw him at the marina this morning. He hired a commercial artist to design a new logo for the back of his yacht with the word Commodore written in gold below the medallion. Pretty cocky."

"So you're really taking off?" I asked.

"Sure am!" Nancy said. "Getting outta Dodge before the would-be Commodores turn the Yacht Club into the OK Corral. I thought about having a T-shirt made that said *No Interest in Being Commodore*, but heading out to sea will be better for my health."

"Are you going to be safe sailing by yourself? Isn't Nevis Island somewhere out in the Caribbean?" Lizzy frowned. "This is pretty sudden news. How long have you been planning this adventure?"

"I'll be hunky-dory. Running a restaurant leaves you with a craving and it ain't for fried fish. I hunger for peace and quiet. Yesterday it hit me. I'm not getting any younger. If I don't go now, I may never make it." If she smirked any harder her lips would pop off.

"I've left papers with my lawyer transferring Crabby Nancy's Fried Fish to Dave if I'm not back within a year. Only thing—Dave can't change the name of my place. There should always be a Crabby Nancy in Starfish Cove. Other than that, it's his from the barstools to the iced tea spoons with access to the bank accounts and the bills."

"Dave never mentioned anything to me. He doesn't know does he?"

"He's about to find out. Don't warn him. Let me have the pleasure of telling him."

She gave Lizzy a wink. "You're going to see even less of him, now kid. He's gonna be working those tight buns off."

While Nancy blathered and Lizzy's eyeballs spun I wrapped two jars of cream in separate sheets of tissue and slipped them into one of our logoed bags.

Nancy ferreted in her purse, pulled out the largest roll of bills I'd ever seen. "Traveling money." She laid down two fifties. "Be well, ladies!" The queen of fried fish grabbed the pink bag and zipped out the door.

"Well I never expected that!" Lizzy said.

We had just enough time to close our gaping jaws when Grams blew in moving faster than the Road Runner with Wile E Coyote on his tail.

She held two pieces of paper in her green-gloved hand. She slammed them on the counter. "Step one in nailing him!"

CHAPTER 11

*G*rams pointed her finger in the air. "The challenger's stage name is Harry Whodunit! He might be a newbie magician out to make a name for himself or a serial challenger."

She dropped her purse on the counter and scrambled onto a stool. She separated the papers. "This is his ad copy and this one is our standard advertising form. He thought he was smart paying cash but his prints should be all over these."

The lady did dress to impress. This time she resembled a leprechaun in a teal and emerald mini dress, black tights, green gloves, and black orthopedic shoes. Her reporter's fedora was pulled down low over her red-rimmed eyes.

"We need to give these to the cops to see if they can match any fingerprints." She favored me with a stern look. "Did Kal's clowns get prints from Nelson's place?"

"They dusted like crazy."

"Good!" she pushed her hat back on her head. "Got a little plastic bag? I'll put these papers in it."

I grabbed a bag meant for samples and slid it across the counter.

Grams slipped the ad forms inside the bag.

"We'll have to tell Kal," I said. "Why we want to process these for prints. He's not going to do it without a reason."

"Make up something. You're trained to persuade people!" In her excitement she slipped off the stool but scampered back on. How many coffees had she swigged since breakfast?

Persuade Kal to run a comparison of prints found in Nelson's apartment with a *Silverfish Gazette* ad copy and order form—but not tell him why? I could improvise with the best of them, but nobody was *that* good.

Lizzy rubbed her temples. "He had to know he was too old to climb out of a dangle."

Grams nodded. "The Masked Dangler had a lot of enemies. Even if Nelson took the challenge seriously, he had more sense than to risk a dangle."

"Okay," I said. "We agree it wasn't an accident while he prepared for the Dangler challenge. What did Harry Whodunit hope to gain by issuing it? The unmasking of Nelson in some way we don't understand yet? Or a shot to break into the big time by default when the reigning dangling master didn't show?"

"You think my father's death didn't have anything to do with Harry Whodunit?"

Grams shook her head. "I don't know how but this challenge is connected to Nelson's death. It walks like a duck and quacks like a murder."

"Running an ad doesn't mean this Whodunit guy set out to kill Nelson," I said. The whole thing felt more like a goose chase than a duck walk.

"I have to find Harry Whodunit! I owe it to my son. Any word from the medical examiner?"

As if on cue, the bell over the door jingled and Kal walked in.

He locked eyes with me. Something was up.

"Hello, ladies. I… I…" He blew out his breath and looked at the ceiling.

"Just let us have it, sonny!" Grams turned on the stool so her back was braced against the counter.

Kal sighed. "The M.E. confirmed his initial diagnosis. Nelson was alive when he hung himself by his heels. He suffered a massive stroke as the blood rushed to his head. He went instantly and didn't suffer. I still don't know how he was able to pull it off."

Grams squinted at Lizzy and then at me—warning us to button our lips.

"It's possible he did it to himself manually," Kal said. "He could have lassoed the chandelier, dropped the rope, tied it around his ankles and pulled himself up."

Grams barked. "Even when he was a whippersnapper dangler he didn't have that kind of strength!"

"A whippersnapper dangler?" Kal stared at Grams. "Dangler? You mean that prank ad in the *Silverfish Gazette*?"

"Senior moment," she muttered, covering her mouth with her hand.

If Kal had been a cartoon character, a light bulb would have come on over his head. He said, "Grams, you're not being straight with me. Your son was the Dangler who was being challenged. Finally this crazy scene makes sense. He was training for the showdown. Foolish thing for a man of his age and in his condition to do and it cost him his life."

"He waited years to become Commodore of the Yacht Club," Lizzy said. "He wouldn't fall for a trick like that challenge and risk what he finally achieved."

"But he did," Kal said. "His ego was legendary. He couldn't help himself."

Grams turned and slipped the plastic bag containing the ad copy and the agreement into her purse. Clearly any chance of cooperating with the police was out the window now that Kal was convinced it was an accident and Grams was certain it was murder.

You could have heard a cotton ball drop, the silence was deafening. Kal's next question might be the deal breaker. We'd have to tell him about Whodunit. Grams returned to her previous position with her back against the counter and her purse held tight.

She and Kal were about to square off. *In this corner, weighing ninety pounds and claiming homicide—*

Just in the nick of time an angel arrived in the form of Ruth Reynolds, one of our best clients. She was *my* excuse to step away. If Grams didn't tell Kal about Harry Whodunit, she'd be withholding an important piece of evidence. I wasn't into guilt by association.

I elbowed Lizzy and raced around the counter to help Ruth. My partner stepped on the backs of my ballet shoes with her clunky wedgies as she fought to distance herself from Grams and Kal.

Lizzy whispered in my ear. "If Grams doesn't tell Kal about Harry Whodunit, I don't want to be a part of her fib by omission. Eventually he's going to find out and be madder than a wet rooster." She raised her hand as if shooing a fly. "I want nothing to do with those two—not now."

"Ruth! How lovely to see you!" I gushed.

Lizzy grabbed a basket of under eye cream from the nearest shelf, and inserted herself between our client and me. Her sales spiels were an art form.

While Lizzy swung into high chat with Ruth, I went into eavesdropping mode. Grams and Kal, although speaking intensely, were keeping their voices down and I could only hear snippets of their conversation. Grams insisted on robbery leading to homicide while Kal was convinced it was a dangling accident.

I slid closer to them. Would Grams tell him about Harry

Whodunit?

"I don't recall seeing an ad like that in the *Silverfish Gazette,*" Grams said, her words dripping with innocence.

"Aren't you in charge of advertising at the *Gazette?*" Kal said.

Grams pushed her fedora down over her brow. "What does it say on my hatband?"

"Reporter." Kal took on the tone of a child answering the school principal.

"So don't be asking me about advertising." Her hat settled over her eyes. "Why don't you just skidaddle?"

Kal turned to me. "Before I forget, I'd like a bar of your lavender soap."

His request came out of nowhere. He'd once bought a jar of cold cream for his mother but other than that...

"We're out of lavender soap," I said. "Come back next week and we'll have a new batch ready."

He cut me a suspicious look. Without a farewell, he turned, nodded at Ruth, and strode across the shop.

"I'll be back!" He didn't slam the door but he didn't close it quietly either.

Grams slipped off her stool, grabbed her purse, and headed to the back room. Beads of sweat dripped from under the brim of her hat.

I waited for Lizzy to finish up with Ruth Reynolds. Sales required a certain amount of theatrics of which my partner possessed more than her share. "Our creams are handmade... shortly before you buy them. You can feel confident they haven't been sitting on a shelf."

With smiles and good wishes Lizzy sent our Ruth off carrying two gift jars of magical cold cream for her nieces plus a fistful of business cards.

"I assume Grams and Kal didn't reach an accord," Lizzy said.

"It looks like she expects her posse to be ready to ride."

CHAPTER 12

Grams paced from one corner of the shop to the other punching her gloved right fist into her left palm. "It's almost noon. Can't you close early? If this Harry Whodunit is any good at magic he's gotta know we're on to him. He's liable to skip town."

"How do we find this guy?" I continued to humor her. "I didn't see an address on the ad copy or form."

"We can pick up his trail at the *Magician's Hat*!" Grams pointed an index finger in the air.

"The *Magician's Hat*?" Was she having another senior moment?

"Don't look at me that way, Olive! It's an old theater where the tricksters hang out. Like Elks or Moose—the illusionists congregate in the *Hat*."

"How come I've never heard of this *Hat*?" Lizzy raised one brow. "I thought I knew all the real estate in and around Starfish Cove."

"The magicians have always kept it a secret. You, like almost everybody else, think it's a welfare facility for the Sheet Metal

Workers and Hair Dressers Union. It's been here since the Depression. Being magicians they can come and go as they please."

That was a little hard to swallow. A secret lasting for decades in this little town? I said, "How do you know about it, Grams?"

"From Nelson. When he was a boy, he did the Boy Scout thing and helped an old magician cross the street. When the guy learned he was fascinated by magic, he took a shine to him and introduced him to the men at the *Magician's Hat*. When I questioned him about where he was going every day after school, he told me but made me promise to keep the secret."

"Is that how Father knew how the illusions were created? The ones he exposed?"

"He kept a journal. I saw it once. Loaded with private information, codes, and ciphers." Tears welled in her eyes. "That's how he made his fortune. I tried many times to stop him. My son the blackmailer."

"Blackmail!" I blurted.

"They'd pay up or he'd expose their specialty illusions. Your average magician doesn't make much money, but Nelson siphoned what he could get—a few hundred here, a few hundred there. He'd have them leave the cash in different places. They never knew who they were paying off."

"I thought Nelson just went about ruining careers—willy-nilly."

"He did that also—as the Masked Dangler. At each dangling performance, he'd reveal the secret of one of the common tricks that are part of every magician's show. This earned the Masked Dangler the hatred of every magician."

Lizzy leaned on the counter, twirling a lock of her hair. "Did my mother know about his slimy career?"

"Nelson was long finished with blackmailing, as well as dangling when he met your mother."

She fumbled in her pocket for a tissue and blew her nose with an unladylike honk. "Nelson hit pay dirt when Silas Lamb took him under his wing."

"He knew Silas Lamb?" I settled on a stool, stunned to know that Lizzy's father was mentored by the greatest magician ever—next to Harry Houdini.

"Nelson could play the young innocent real well. When he wasn't the Masked Dangler, he acted as a part-time assistant for Silas. He worked for him until he knew all the great man's secrets, which ended up as a two-way street. Silas learned Nelson was the Masked Dangler."

Lizzy appeared dazed when she said, "How do you know that, Grams?"

"Just happened to overhear an argument between them when Silas stopped by the house one evening. Silas was soon to leave on a world tour culminating in making the Eiffel Tower disappear. Evidently Nelson thought it was the perfect time to threaten to reveal all of Silas' illusions unless Silas paid him to keep quiet."

I was confused. "But Silas had something on Nelson. He knew he was the Masked Dangler."

"Exposing Nelson would only result in less revenue at the dangling events. Part of the reason for his popularity was the mysteriousness. But exposing Silas' secrets would destroy his world tour and end his career."

A blip was on my radar screen. "When did this happen relative to the last dangle in paradise?"

Grams smiled at me. "I knew you'd ask that. Two nights after their argument, Nelson was shot in the arena—not in the arena—in the shoulder in the arena. And yes, I suspected Silas but didn't say anything to the police because it would have exposed Nelson as a blackmailer. My son wasn't hurt badly and was adamant that I keep my mouth shut about everything."

I pressed my finger under my chin and closed my gaping mouth. "Did any one suspect Silas?"

"No reason to. As far as anyone knew, Silas was Nelson's mentor and there were no problems between them. Silas split for Europe the following day to start his tour."

She honked again. Grams had a lot of wind for a small woman.

"Nelson was in the hospital overnight. The discharging doctor told him not to operate any heavy machinery. So being his only friend *and* his mother, I drove him on his errands the next day. He was hot to get to The First Bank of Starfish Cove. He ordered me to sit in the lobby while he met with the manager. My son thought he was so clever."

I reached over and closed Lizzy's mouth with my one-finger chin-lift.

"He was up to something. I pretended to search for the bank's powder room. That's when I happened to overhear Nelson talking to the manager—wasn't easy cause the office door was closed and I had to press my ear against it." Grams shook her head. "Two million was wired to Nelson's account right after the shooting!"

"Silas?" I asked.

Grams nodded. "Had to be. Silas couldn't let Nelson go public with his secrets and probably thought that by paying off, Nelson wouldn't suspect he was the shooter. At age twenty-one my son had a small fortune and an army of locals who hated him for his attitude. Remember that was back when a million bucks was still a million bucks. Nelson covered it by bragging about inheriting a fortune and lording it over folks. The rest is history."

The circle in this tale was closing. "I've seen stories that Silas died under suspicious circumstances doing a trick."

"His first international performance became his last. Silas' most remarkable illusion was cutting himself in half. This time the stunt was more successful than he expected. He died on stage at the London Coliseum."

Grams studied her gloves unable to face us for long minutes. Finally she looked up. "The investigation revealed someone tampered with Silas' props probably *before* they were shipped overseas. My son told me he was afraid Silas would make another attempt on his life when he returned from Europe."

A huge tear rolled out of her eye. "A child is a mother's greatest pleasure but can also be her greatest burden."

The bell over the door jangled.

I squinted, the glare of sunlight caused my eyes to water. The hazy figure looked like Lizzy coming in—but it couldn't be because she was standing next to me.

Our visitor dashed from the door to Grams. She lifted the elderly lady from her seat with one hand. "Oh Grams! I am so sorry for you!"

Lizzy ran around the counter and joined the hug-a-thon. "Pam! My sweet baby sister—why does it take something so awful to bring us together? I missed you!"

The three ladies wept, but in my professional opinion it was more about reuniting than the loss of Nelson Dingler.

Pam was a miniature of Lizzy with pixie-cut honey-brown hair and the same amber eyes as her grandmother and sister. The diminutive gal kept her nurse's strength hidden under a pale blue T-shirt, black yoga pants, and white Sketchers. The strap of a gym bag crossed over her shoulder.

"You must be Olive. Finally we meet!" If possible her smile was even wider than Lizzy's. Pam embraced me in slender muscular arms.

She glanced around the shop. One would never guess she was here to sort through her father's last days. "Nice. I like it. Very feminine. Thanks for sending me the cold cream. I shared it with a few friends and now have a dozen orders for you to fill. The entire staff of the E.R. is crazy for Nonna's cream."

Pam grabbed Lizzy in a one-handed hug and continued to study our shop. A frown formed on her brow. "Too bad you don't have a table by the window. We could sit while we talk and watch the cars go by."

Maybe Ivy was right. Should we reconsider tableside beverage service? I shuddered.

Releasing her grip on her sister Pam pulled a stool over. The four of us grouped near the counter.

"Without coloring the story," Pam said, "give me the specifics about our father's demise. I'll come to my own conclusions."

She was the complete opposite of Lizzy who dealt in whimsy and suppositions. Pam hit the ground running like the triage nurse she was. I expected her to pull a blood pressure bracelet from her bag and cuff us.

"Your father was found hanging by his feet from the chandelier in his apartment," Grams said. "The medical examiner says he had a stroke from the blood rushing to his head."

Pam peered at Grams as if the older woman spoke a foreign language. "Why was he hanging upside down?"

"I think he was murdered. Lots of reasons—robbery, revenge, hobbies." Grams held up three fingers going for four.

"Hobbies?" Pam looked dumbfounded.

"We never told you about Nelson's secret life," Grams said, lowering her voice.

Pam put her finger to her grandmother's lips. "Just the facts. We'll get to that later."

"Pam, you won't understand unless you get some background," I said, giving her my *professional psychologist look*. "I can understand you want to layout your own chart for your father but trust me— you can't do it without his full history.

Walking behind the counter I pulled out the copy of the *Silverfish Gazette*. "You have to know what we're dealing with." I pointed to the magician's ad.

Grams stepped away from the cluster of stools. She adjusted her leprechaun dress, handed her fedora to Lizzy. "See that ad? In his younger years, your father was the Masked Dangler, he also dabbled in blackmail."

"You are so bed-panning me," Pam laugh-snorted. "My father—our father—wouldn't risk his life at any age. He was a misogynistic coward. If he were here, I'd tell him that to his face."

Pam gave me the squint eye. "And the medical examiner said—"

"Natural by unnatural causes."

"I'm not believing this. Grams, tell me again." Pam rubbed her forehead. "Don't leave anything out."

Grams recited her son's history. I could pretty much deliver the story by heart.

Pam stepped to the front window. She stood in silence with her back to us. Then suddenly spun on her rubber heels. "Okay. I'm in. Let's track down this magician." She checked her watch. "The sign on your door says three, but can you close early? The sooner the better."

They all looked at me for an okay. "Sure. We can close now. It's not like it's the first time. I just hope it's the last."

CHAPTER 13

"It's down here somewhere, maybe in the next alley," Grams mumbled. We let her drive because she had the biggest car. It was a mistake. The Edsel took the corners like a Barcalounger—up the curb and down the curb. One large green trashcan survived, the rest rolled over in the alley like bowling pins as she hit them bing, bang, bong.

"That's it!" Grams barked. "Ain't been here since Nelson—" She brushed her cheek with her left hand, her gloved right gripped the skinny steering wheel—the size of a hula-hoop. Looking over her shoulder, Grams turned the wheel twice and zipped the Edsel into a space I could have sworn wouldn't fit a compact car.

I stepped onto the sidewalk with the trio of Dinglers at my side. Eyeing the steps that led down below street level I wondered how the place remained for so long after the many hurricanes and floods—routine for the area.

Pausing at the head of the stairs I admired the antique sign over the door. The Sheet Metal Workers and Hair Dressers Union radiated the aura of 1930s workers' social hall.

I turned to the group and whispered, "We might not get a warm welcome here—and not just because they're a reclusive bunch."

Pam rubbed her forehead. "Why not? I don't get it. I guess I'm a bit overwhelmed with everything I've learned in the past few hours. These magicians don't know Father was the Masked Dangler."

"His death has been all over the media so they know he died in the position similar to a dangle and that the Masked Dangler was challenged to compete at the Magician's Fusion event. They may be worried about being suspects in his death. Harry Whodunit, in particular."

Pam shook her head, like clearing cobwebs. "Let's go find out."

"It might be better if none of you used your real names."

"I have nothing to hide," Grams shook her head. "It's these quackers that have something to do with Nelson's demise."

Grams' gang clomped down the weathered stone steps with me in the lead. Pam struggled to help her stubborn grandmother. Lizzy brought up the rear.

A firm believer in acting first and apologizing later, I didn't bother to knock—just yanked the heavy wooden door open. It groaned in protest.

We stepped inside. The room was dimly lit and smelled of mold and cigars. My stomach roiled.

Before I could adjust my eyes to the darkness, my shoe caught on the edge of a carpet and I pitched forward breaking my fall with the flat of my hands. My face pressed against a ratty oriental rug loaded with years of dirty tricks. I scrambled to my feet spitting and sputtering.

The buzz of magician conversation fell into silence. All eyes were on us—or so it seemed. It took a minute to adjust to the gritty darkness. I blinked and then studied the room and its occupants.

Leather armchairs lit by the glow of mismatched Arts and

Crafts style lamps held men in black—ranging in age from old to very old. Magazines were stacked on a coffee table the size of a coffin. Ashtrays littered end tables.

The wall to our right was lined with framed photos of guys pulling rabbits from hats, grasping fluttering doves, or holding hands with a Vanna White assistant. Below each frame hung a cheesy brass plaque with born and died dates. We'd stepped into an outtake from the Adams Family.

A jaggedy row of weak footlights illuminated a small stage at the back of the room. Were they auditioning new members? From what I could see they needed some young blood. The whipper-snappers in the place were probably Vaudeville alumni.

A flickering spotlight cast a beam on an oversized dartboard hanging near the stage.

Plastered on the target was a large tattered photo of the Masked Dangler, shoes up.

Two senior men approached us. One wore a black tie ensemble and appeared ready to go on stage. The other wore a formal T-shirt printed with the faded image of a tuxedo and appeared ready to perform on a street corner.

"Can we help you?" Black Tie asked. He smirked. We were clearly no threat as demonstrated by my entrance.

"What he really means," T-Shirt said, "is can we help you out the door? This is a private club."

"We're looking for Harry Whodunit," I said.

T-shirt's face contorted into a crooked smile as he talked out of the side of his mouth. "Don't recognize the name. Is he a sheet metal worker or a hair dresser?"

This guy could rile a Buddhist monk. "He's a magician."

"Black Tie snorted. "You're in the wrong place if you're looking for a magician."

Grams piped up. "Listen, sonny, I was living in this burg when you were just a gleam in your daddy's eye. I don't care what your sign says. This is the Magician's Hat and I work for the *Gazette*. Whodunit placed an ad with us so when we decided we wanted a magician for a party, I thought of him and figured this is the place to find him."

Black Tie straightened up like Grams had just whacked him with her gigantic purse.

All the magicians within earshot turned their attention our way.

She took a step forward into his personal space. "Don't try to shine on me. My boy used to hang out here years ago."

"Your b…boy," Black Tie sputtered. "Who's that?"

"Nelson Dingler."

"I remember him. Nasty piece of work." T-shirt continued to speak out of the side of his mouth. "He quit coming around after Silas bought the farm. Guess his mentor

cashing out doing a trick crushed his drive to make magic a career. Probably the smart move anyway. We're all hand-to-mouth and he's a big shot businessman. Well, was a big shot businessman. Sorry for your loss, lady."

Sorry my eye. Grams told us the local magicians hated Nelson because of his mean nature. "Back to Whodunit," I said. "Is he around?"

T-shirt glanced over his shoulder in the direction of the dart-board. "You ladies looking to hire a magician? He reached in the pocket of his jeans and pulled out a business card. "Name's Bottom —Bart Bottom. I'm available for weddings and funerals. I do a mean strip for bachelorette parties."

Now that was a visual. "Maybe he thought I wouldn't notice he had avoided answering my question. I slipped the card in my pocket, cooties and all. "What's with the picture on the dartboard?"

"That's magician business, not your business."

Maybe it wasn't the dartboard that Bart Bottom looked at. A body slouched in a chair near it, a copy of *Variety* covering his face.

Either he was practicing reading in the dark or hiding. It was time to turn the entertainment over to Lizzy and get on with the investigation.

I gave my partner a subtle wink. "Lizzy, you can best explain what we need for our show."

Without hesitation Lizzy ran with it. She pushed her long curls away from her face. She licked her bottom lip and did that thing she does with her eyes. Men turn into dodos when she does the lip-eye thing. It's her secret weapon.

With a faint nod Pam reined in Grams. I was free to snoop.

Bottom, Black Tie, and the rest of the magicians—all except the *Variety* guy—focused on Lizzy as she put her hands on her hips, re-licked her lips, and threw in a wiggle. Even in the dim light she had them enthralled.

I inched my way over to the *Variety* reader and sat on the arm of his chair.

He didn't budge, so I tugged at his magazine.

The guy peeked at me nervously over the top of the pages. He was young—much younger than his cohorts—and telegraphed vulnerability to intimidation.

"Harry Whodunit?"

"Who's asking?" he said, his Poirot mustache loosened on one side. His Buddy Holly glasses had no lenses.

"I have a few questions. Suggest you keep the paper up, wouldn't want your colleagues getting the wrong impression—you look scared stupid. Or maybe that should be you look scared, stupid."

Harry pouted, sending his moustache into his lap. "You've no right to question me. Nothing wrong in a little advertising."

I was right. He was afraid his ad would connect him with Dingler's dangling death.

He pointed his chin at the rest of Grams' gang. "Isn't that Lizzy Kelly? Ain't she a Dingler? Is that why you're poking around?"

Clarity smacked him in the face. His eyes popped so large his Buddy Holly's slid down his nose. "Dingler *was* the Dangler! My daddy was right!"

I put my hand on his shoulder pinning him to his seat. "I didn't say Dingler was the Dangler. Your ad may have incited someone to commit a dangling-type homicide and the police might think that makes you an accessory. If you want us to keep you out of it, you need to begin cooperating right now starting with who's your daddy?"

Harry's complexion went from chalky to red. I pushed the right button.

"My daddy doesn't have anything to do with it. These old guys are always talking about the Masked Dangler like he thought he was better than any magician ever." He shrugged. I wondered if he was real. Maybe I could bring him out of hiding. It was just one darn ad."

"Let's go outside and get us some privacy. My friends have questions for you."

"I've seen that old lady before. She's a tough cookie. I'd rather just talk to you."

"They're my posse—they get to decide whether we call in the cops. That ad could cost you more than a couple of bucks." I stood aside and motioned him to precede me.

I gave Lizzy my *enough* look and she shut off her flirting with a twitch of her nose. A quick nod to Grams and Pam and they understood we had our man.

Grams waved off Lizzy's fan club and headed up the stairs, followed by Pam and Lizzy.

As Harry and I stepped out the door, a phlegmy voice called from the dimness. "Hey Marchmain! How about paying your tab?"

Rex Marchmain was the person Nancy warned us about!

Harry stopped so suddenly I almost slammed into him. I said, "Is Rex Marchmain your father?"

He turned around and said, "Be back after I take care of my bill. The skinny dude in black dashed past me into the *Hat*. This wasn't about paying his tab the magician was pulling a vanishing act.

Obviously familiar with the layout of the joint, Harry ran through the murky clubroom without a stumble or bumble. He leapt onto the stage, went into a full body slide on the wooden floor and slipped under the musty velveteen curtain.

I dropped to the floor and rolled under the curtain after him— coming up on the dark side of the drape.

CHAPTER 14

"Marchmain!" I screamed, scrambling to my feet. A blue, red, and yellow phone booth loomed over me. The top of the booth was painted with an evil man-in-the-moon face and chipped golden letters spelling *Vanish*.

I was in some sort of backstage storage area crammed with medieval torture devices, a rack of capes, and a couple of sets of mannequin legs—props for cutting a lady in two.

The sound of running and then a door slamming told me Harry Whodunit had escaped. The kid was not worth stubbing my toes tramping through this hoarders' habitat. He was a Marchmain and would be easy enough to find in Starfish Cove.

A chunk of grit lodged in the corner of my eye. I was in the process of blinking it out when Lizzy crawled under the curtain.

"Are you okay?" she grabbed my shoulder.

"MRI."

She gave me the once over. "You're hurt?"

"Mascara Related Injury. I'll blink it out."

"So that was Harry Whodunit? He must be guilty of something if he ran."

"Lift up this darn thing!" Grams barked from the opposite side of the drape. "Have you got the Phantom of the Opera back there?"

"Here you go!" Lizzy and I grabbed the musty roller at the bottom of the curtain and hefted it high enough so Grams could crawl through.

"Where's Pam?" Lizzy asked.

I peeked under the curtain but she wasn't on the stage.

"She lit out the front door. That gal's got nurse's legs. She's faster than me!" Grams grinned. "Even money says she catches Whodunit."

My vision finally clear, I traipsed after Lizzy and Grams making our way through a wonderland of props. Dark blue cloths covered many of the obstacles—their shapes hinting at what lay beneath. We skirted around a unicycle, a carton of wands, an invisible head wearing a derby, and an empty cage with rabbit droppings.

We found the unlit exit Harry used to escape. I tugged it open and we stepped out into the sunlight.

Lizzy elbowed me and I turned to the left looking up the alley towards the street.

Pam stood on the cobblestones, her feet spread apart in a cop stance. She'd pinned Harry against a brick wall with her hands on his throat.

The kid squirmed in a vain attempt to escape the nurse's grip. I made a mental note to ask Pam for lessons.

"Just who do you think you're messing with, sonny?" Grams came at him. Her shoulders hunched, her gloved fists knotted, and her eyes blazed. "We got you! Why'd you taunt the Masked Dangler?"

Pam's hands garbled Harry's plea. "Keep that old lady away... from... me!" He squeaked out the words.

"Rex Marchmain's your father!" I wedged myself between Grams and Harry.

71

"He's not! Never heard of him."

"Your cover's blown, Marchmain." I gave him the boxer's stare-down. "We're taking you to your father. I read minds and mine is telling me we can find him at the Yacht Club."

Harry's body went limp—an involuntary sign of submission. "I'll tell you the whole thing, just don't take me to my daddy—I mean father!"

Rex Marchmain must be one scary guy.

Pam loosened her grip, while Grams poked the kid in his skinny ribs. "Okay. Talk. What's with the ad?"

"As I told the blonde," he said, pointing to me. "The old guys at the *Hat* made a legend out of him. I figured knowing his tricks might help me get a foot up in the business. I was just guessing about Dingler. I don't have any idea who the Masked Dangler is— honest. Honest!"

It was that extra honest that told me the kid was lying like a rug.

Harry cringed looking at Grams. She bared her choppers as if she wanted to chew his face off.

A car drove slowly across the entrance to the alley. It stopped. The driver stared at us. We made an odd sight—three youngish women and a granny mugging a skinny young dude. The man behind the wheel shrugged and continued driving. Peculiar things were always going on in Starfish Cove. It was safer to mind your P's and Q's.

Resignation passed over Harry's face like a rain cloud. Rescue was not in his horoscope. "I'm practicing to be a dangler," he said by way of an excuse.

His bogus claim wasn't going to save him. I gave him the boxer's stare again.

He tried to stare back then looked at his feet. "I figured I could beat the Masked Dangler and take the title from him. I even bought a mask—I was that certain. An old dude bound to flop at the Dangle Off—or chicken out!"

"You can't make a living dangling. That went out with Ed Sullivan."

"Don't know him either!" the kid whined.

All of Grams' gang rolled their eyes simultaneously. Dumb as the dirt on the carpet inside the *Hat*.

The door squeaked open and Bart Bottom stuck his head out.

"If you're gonna kill him, don't do it in the alley. Twenty bucks if you drop him off the pier and take a video. I'll throw in a free striptease."

The kid yelped. "Stop joking around and help me. They're gonna drag me to the Yacht Club!"

"Nice knowing you" Bottom said and closed the door with a thud.

Harry put up a good fight—more like a greased pig tussle, but he was no match for Pam. She held his right arm in a wrestler's hold and duck-marched him to Grams' car.

"I ain't getting in no Edsel. What if somebody sees me?"

"There's nothing wrong with an Edsel!" Grams snapped. "Goldie has over two hundred thousand miles on her and hasn't had an oil change in two years. Drives like a dream."

Harry put his hands over his face, accepted his fate and allowed Pam to stuff him into the backseat between her and Lizzy. I rode shotgun.

Our cruise was uneventful aside from one minor fender bender with an ownerless parked car.

"Reach in the glove box, Olive." Grams said. She pulled two car lengths up from the dented car and kept the Edsel's engine idling —striving, not idling. "See that stack of pink cards? Get one and slip it under his windshield wiper."

The pink cards all bore the same printed message.

SORRY I HIT YOU BUT IT WAS YOUR FAULT FOR PARKING THERE.
NEXT TIME BE MORE CAREFUL.
~ A FRIEND

No name. No phone. No sugar coating. But the act of leaving a note impressed the bystanders.

We rattled exactly six minutes from the *Hat* to the marina—I know this because the dial clock on the ancient dashboard counted off the time in little lurches. I needed an oil change too.

The blue and white roof of the Yacht Club came into sight. Time to meet Mr. Rex Marchmain.

CHAPTER 15

A paunchy salt-and-pepper haired man wearing a navy-blue blazer with SCYC embroidered in gold thread on the breast pocket was slouching against the wall. He snapped to attention when he saw us approaching and stood in front of the door.

Grams stepped ahead of us and said, "I'll handle this."

The doorman smiled. "How can I help you ladies? Are you meeting one of the members?"

She put her fists on hips. "Are you saying you don't recognize me, Freddy? I've known you since you were in diapers."

He squinted and recognition swept across his face. "Mrs. Dingler. I'm so sorry. The peepers aren't what they used to be."

Freddy opened the door and with a bow and a sweeping gesture ushered Grams' gang into the yacht club with Harry wedged in the middle subdued by a wristlock sometimes called a come-along by police—deftly administered by Pam.

"Let's try the bar first. Happy hour should've started by now," Lizzy said.

Harry tried to break free of Pam's grip. "Don't throw me in the barrrrr!" The word bar dragged out as Pam increased the wristlock pressure. His begging sounded a bit like Brer Rabbit.

His father had to be a terror. My stomach did a little squish-squash. I hated making scenes but sometimes it couldn't be helped.

The bar smelled like cigars with a light overlay of diesel fuel that drifted in the open sliders. The room itself was posh with pale blue walls, oak framed pictures of distinguished looking men, and blue plaid carpet. A huge sailfish arched over the mirrored back of the bar. He might once have been real but was more likely of the fiberglass species.

Wraparound windows offered a panoramic view of the marina. I shuddered from the memory of a recent murder on these docks.

A dandified youngish man dressed in yachting attire rose from a bar stool. Tall, thin, and handsome in an F. Scott Fitzgerald way, he stepped toward us. He wore a light blue blazer, blue and white pinstripe shirt, cream-colored slacks and boat shoes.

As he drew close I got a better look at him. Cut close on the sides, his bottle blonde hair dipped over his tanned brow. He'd had more than a nip and tuck judging from his lizard-like mouth and hyper-raised brows. I adjusted my guestimate of his age and put him on the far side of fifty, maybe far enough to reach sixty.

"Rex Marchmain." He extended his hand in the general direction of our group—no one took it. "I see you have my son. Now what has he done? Broken a window? A fender bender?"

Marchmain's eyes fell on Grams. "Mrs. Dingler!" He spoke in a clipped accent—British by way of Connecticut. "I'm so sorry to hear about your son. Nelson and I weren't close but he was an impressive man—worthy of the position of Commodore of the finest yacht club on the west coast of Florida. Is there anything I can do?"

I was expecting *Monster Trucks on Ice*, and instead we got *Bridget Jones Diary*.

He directed his attention to Lizzy. "I believe you're Nelson

Dingler's daughter—Elizabeth? I'm sorry to hear about your father." Leaning in, he took her hand and held it.

Lizzy yanked free. One brow shot up. She was having none of his act.

He turned his charm on Pam. "You must be the youngest Dingler daughter, Pamela. I see the resemblance. I can't help but notice you have my son in a wristlock."

"We believe he may know something about Nelson Dingler's death." I extended my hand. "I'm Olive Peroni—family friend."

"Ah, the cold cream mogul. A pleasure to meet you." Marchmain's hand was dry, rough, and warm. His voice sounded like velvet if cloth could talk. I tried not to let Nancy's warning affect my judgment.

"My son is deeply common." Rex wrinkled his lizard lips as if smelling cooking cabbage. "I apologize for whatever he's done. If he's broken anything I will pay for it. If he's offended any of you, he will beg your forgiveness." He glared at his boney offspring. "But as far as having anything to do with the death of anyone— that's impossible."

Pam released Harry, who slumped like a marionette with cut strings.

All controlled charm, Rex Marchmain was clearly running to replace the newly deceased Nelson Dingler.

Every man in Starfish Cove who owned a diesel fueled boat wanted to be Commodore. The life expectancy of yacht club skippers was slightly less than a carnival goldfish in a dinky glass globe and yet these men fought like barracudas for the post.

Was Marchmain capable of murder in order to become the next Commodore? His son was a fool, but was he a tool or operating on his own? Harry placed the ad but did his father set the scheme in motion? Were they hands-on in the strangle-dangle or just criminally negligent for publishing the challenge? They didn't exchange looks, usually a sign of conspiracy.

Marchmain motioned to the dock. "Shall we sit outside and sort out whatever this idiot has done? I'm sure I can make it right."

He made a move to take Grams arm, but she yanked away. With an expression that was neither a smile nor a smirk, he guided us out the double glass doors and onto the deck.

We were escorted to a large round table under one of the awnings. Marchmain snapped his fingers and Harry pulled out a chair. None of the Dinglers accepted Harry's proffered seat so I plunked myself down, while the others each took a chair.

My eyes flit from Rex to Harry as the *sorting out* began.

CHAPTER 16

*G*rams pulled off her gloves—right then left. Her movements were slow and deliberate. She knit her fingers together as if about to 'church and steeple' but instead she cracked her knuckles. The sound made me shiver.

She fixed on Marchmain ignoring Harry. "You want to make right by your son who's a scoundrel. Up until yesterday I too had a scoundrel son." She blinked back her tears.

Marchmain's brow crumpled. "Word is *your* son died from natural causes while hanging from his chandelier. What does that have to do with *my* son?" He glanced at Harry and then returned to Grams. "I thought maybe you had a complaint about his magic stunts—making buildings disappear or swallowing rabbits or whatever? The kid's a menace."

"Your son placed an ad in the *Silverfish Gazette!*" Grams cracked her knuckles again.

"He's over eighteen, is there an age requirement for advertising in that rag?"

The word *rag* just secured Marchmain a lasting enemy in the form of Grams Dingler—ninety pounds of fury.

79

"*The Silverfish Gazette* is not a rag! It placed in the top... mumble...of neighborhood newspapers!"

A sarcastic laugh escaped Marchmain's lizard-like mouth. The only thing missing was a long skinny tongue flicking in and out.

"Mr. Marchmain we believe there is a connection to my father's unnatural natural death with a challenge your son placed in the *Silverfish Gazette*," Lizzy said. "I'm not at liberty to give you the details but we need to know *why* he placed the ad. We have proof he did it."

"What's the big deal?" The velvet in Marchmain's voice turned to sandpaper. He turned to Harry. "Apologize for placing the ad and then make yourself useful on my boat!"

Harry popped from his seat. "Sorry I placed the ad! I'll never advertise again." He reached in his back pocket and took out one of his flyers. He flipped the many-folded piece of paper on the table as if it was a peace offering.

Pam reached out to grab him. "Wait! You haven't answered our questions!"

Harry turned and galloped down the deck towards the marina.

"Let him go. We know where to find him and his daddy," I said, peppering my words with sarcasm.

Marchmain shrugged at Lizzy. It was a conspiratorial motion designed to win her to his side. She ignored it.

"If we find out Nelson's death," Grams said in an icy voice, "had anything to do with your dodo son's challenge, guess who moves to the top of our list of suspects!" The icy tone of Grams' voice sent a chill wiggling down my spine.

"Come on Lizzy. We've got work to do," I said. I nodded at Marchmain. "We'll be in touch."

The would-be Commodore cut me a chilling look.

We piled into Grams' Edsel, a silent prayer for safety of pedestrians and green trashcans on my lips.

Once back at the shop I collected the customer notes slipped through the mail slot while Grams and Pam sat in their cars at the edge of the parking lot ready to pull onto Starfish Boulevard.

Lizzy stood at my side as I gathered the slips of paper. "Anything important?"

There were four order slips and a note from Kal. "I'll sort them out. You take care of your company. See you at my place by six? We must knock out at least two dozen bars of soap tonight." I stuffed the notes in my purse.

Lizzy cut her eyes to Grams and Pam, their engines idling. "WonderDog will need to be walked. Then I have to catch and cage my finches. Pam thinks they're dirty, won't sleep on my sofa until they're locked up. Can you imagine that? I'll order in some dinner for everybody then head to your place."

Kal's note was burning a hole in my purse. He'd sent a text message but there was nothing in the subject line and nothing in the body. Technology...ugh.

I pulled off the boulevard into a service station and fished the note out of my purse. Short and to the point it read— *I must have a bar of your lavender soap from your most recent batch. I can't stress the importance.*

CHAPTER 17

I scanned the parking lot beneath Sandy Shores Towers before pulling into my assigned space. With any luck I could avoid Ivy. The *we-ness* of her letter felt like an anvil on my shoulders. I'd have to be gentle in extricating her nose from Nonna's Cold Cream but I wasn't in the mood for nice tonight.

No sign of Myron's car—maybe he and Ivy were out for early bird dinner. A blessing.

Old mobsters don't retire—they eat early and spend their evenings annoying people.

I grabbed my purse, and dashed up the stairs avoiding the elevator—a neighbor magnet. A note in Ivy's handwriting stuck in my doorjamb, a sneaky way to see if I'd come home. After I locked the door behind me, I poked the note back in the crack between the door and the frame.

Puff lifted her head acknowledging my return with a disdainful look. She held it for a second—just long enough to let me know I'd been a neglectful mother.

The white fur ball jumped off the sofa and scrambled to rub my ankles. I picked her up. "Sorry sweetie. You wouldn't believe the day I've had." Gently placing her on the floor, I refreshed her water and began to set out her food chattering as I worked.

She listened attentively, finally losing her cool. She batted at my leg—which was cat- speak for stop stalling.

I scooped salmon paté into her dish, shaping it into a perfect mound.

The little princess sniffed, flicked her paw at the fish, and scratched as if burying something foul. I didn't have to be a cat therapist to understand.

Puff walked to the pantry, stood on her hind legs and pawed at the door. She was in the mood for kibble. I replaced the fishy salmon with dry cat food. She gobbled it down, sipped some water, and made a beeline for her litter pan.

A bit rubbery, my two-day-old Greek salad became a quick nosh. I rinsed my empty plate and put it in the dishwasher.

Within minutes I was setting up the ingredients for soap making. I spread brown paper over the countertop, lined up the rectangle-shaped soap molds, the container of unscented soap base, lavender essential oils, and a jar of finely crushed lavender.

The flowers had come from Digby's Bee Farm. After I picked a bushel last month, I used a mortar and pestle to crush the blossoms into a fine paste and let it dry.

If we worked fast, Lizzy and I could have a batch cooled and wrapped by morning. Kal would have to be patient. He did say most recent batch, but this would have to suffice.

I kept two bars of the first batch of soap sealed in Tupperware to be used for consistency. All new batches must match that original. Customers who bought lavender soap in June should expect the exact same fragrance and color as the soap they bought in March. Very scientific. Maybe I should wear a white lab coat.

Puff returned, leaped to one of the chairs and studied me with her big blue eyes.

"Want to smell the soap?" I took the lid off and offered it to her. She sneezed.

Staring at the soap in the plastic container it struck me that I had the lavender soap Kal wanted.

"I've got to call Kal!" I yelled scaring Puff off her perch. "He must be trying to match the killer's soap to our lavender soap!"

Puff stood on the floor not sure whether to dart or stay. She leaned against the baseboard and gave me the humans-are-crazy look that only cats can muster.

Kal answered on the second ring.

"I'm at home. Are you nearby?" A tremor betrayed my nerves.

He hesitated. "Is this a trap?"

"I found a bar of lavender soap. You wanted it and I'm guessing why." I looked at the kitchen clock. "Can you get here in the next ten minutes, pick up the soap, and leave right away?"

At times Lizzy seemed uneasy about my bond with Kal. A sixth sense told me it would be best if she didn't find him hanging out at my place when she arrived.

"That's pretty urgent. Got a heavy date?"

I didn't answer.

"I'll be right there."

The kitchen clock read five-fifty. I could count on Lizzy to be late, it was a part of her DNA. She was always late.

I slipped the soap in a plastic bag and zipped it tight.

A quick floss and brush of my teeth, a comb through my hair, and cool damp cloth over my face was all I could accomplish before the doorbell rang.

Kal stood framed in the peephole.

I clicked open the door and stuffed the plastic bag with the bar of soap in his hands. He returned the favor by sticking me with Ivy's note. "This was in your door. Don't I get to come in?"

"Take the soap." I tossed Ivy's note on the small table near the door.

"What's the rush?" Kal tucked the bagged soap in his jacket pocket and pushed into the foyer looking about, an odd expression on his face—curiosity with maybe a tinge of jealousy.

"You can't come in. Lizzy's due here any minute. I don't want her to think we're working together behind her back. I forgot to tell her about the soap on the rope—no big secret. I just forgot."

Kal eased his way farther into the foyer.

"This is one of my comparison bars. I didn't have any at the shop because a guy bought it all while Ivy was babysitting the store."

"When," Kal said, "was Ivy working at the shop?"

"She was there because Lizzy and I took a day trip to Miami so it was the day Dingler died. Ivy said the customer wanted it for wedding favors."

"One person bought your entire inventory of soap. Did that strike you as odd, even suspicious? Especially after you knew there was soap on the rope that killed Dingler? You should have told me sooner."

"I should have told you what sooner? That we had a run on our soap? You want me to call you tomorrow and report how many jars of cold cream we sold?" He could be so irritating. "And speaking of withholding, how long have you suspected the soap on the rope is ours? Obviously, before you stopped in this morning."

"I suspected your soap was a match." Kal said. "The lab found small pieces of crushed flowers."

Lizzy appeared in the doorway with WonderDog at her side, a puzzled expression on her face. "What's going on? What's this about our soap?"

The history between Kal and Lizzy going back to high school days didn't account for their reactions. They were both acting as if we'd been caught canoodling.

"We're going to put our cards on the coffee table." I motioned my guests to the living room.

CHAPTER 18

*L*izzy sat in an armchair, dropping her purse to the floor. The bag hit with a thud.

Kal took the sofa. I hovered unable to sit, ready to clear up all the half-forgotten clues and one-sided secrets.

WonderDog lay on his back at Lizzy's feet while Puff scrambled onto his belly teasing at his chest hairs. The pets were comfortable—it was time to sort out the humans.

"Why didn't you tell me about the soap on the rope?" Lizzys eyes were locked on me.

"I honestly forgot. So much happened at once—Grams insisted on tracking down the killer and then the *Magician's Hat* and chasing Harry Whodunit." I smacked my palms at my sides. "I'm sorry I just plain forgot."

Kal leaned forward, his long legs reaching the coffee table and his hands on his knees. "The *Magician's Hat?* Harry Whodunit? What is *that* all about? If there *is* a killer Grams is bound to get in his way."

WonderDog leaped to attention at the sound of Lizzy sighing. Puff tumbled off him, dropped to the floor, and swatted at his tail.

"It's okay, WonderDog." She gave her hound a gentle smile.

Satisfied his beloved mistress wasn't in pain, the dog turned and poked his snoot at Puff. A cat and dog chase ensued, which allowed us to get back to business.

"Does that dangle challenge have something to do with Nelson's death? Are you gals withholding more evidence?" He gave us an exaggerated stern look. "I'm going to have to take you both to jail unless you fess up."

With a shrug, I fessed up first and Lizzy followed. By the time we finished Kal was scowling and was back to the darn soap. "A stranger bought all your lavender soap on the day Nelson died? That bit of information tied to the soap on a rope is important? You're going to have some serious explaining to do."

"We couldn't know yesterday that there was a connection. If my nose hadn't been stuffed with fingerprint powder I probably would've smelled the lavender."

The timing rolled around in my mind like a billiard ball on an empty pool table. "We didn't even know about the soap sale until we read Ivy's list in the shop—the day *after* Nelson's death."

Lizzy and I exchanged looks. "Ivy should be able to describe the soap buyer. It's almost as if someone is trying to frame us."

I chewed on my lip as I watched WonderDog and Puff play. Their innocent nips and yips were strangely soothing. They finally settled in one giant ball of fur, adjusting their positions until they were comfortable. Why can't people be more like animals—a little tussle and then a nap?

Lizzy and Kal remained silent. I struggled to fill in the gaps.

"I'll track Ivy down tomorrow. I'm not up to dealing with her tonight—especially if Myron's around. By morning he'd have his New York goon squad on their way here—if they can break out of their senior care facility.

I'd have to face Ivy sooner or later, the latter being my preference. It's never fun bursting bubbles but the lady presumed too much. *Nonna's Cold Cream* didn't need Macy's business plan or her extreme giveaways.

I glanced at Nonna's antique clock. Time got away from us. Almost eight. There'd be no soap making tonight.

"I'll trade with you," Lizzy said. "You tell Grams that Kal made us talk. I'll get the description of the soap buyer from Ivy."

"Chicken! Afraid of your own Grams?"

She reddened.

"You're not capable of refusing Ivy—not with your soft heart. You'll let her bring all her wonderful Macy's experience to bear and we'll end up with a little shop of horrors. Nope. I'll handle Ivy. You break the news to Grams."

"If you get a description from Ivy text it to me," Kal said. "He's probably not a local as she knows everyone in Starfish Cove and would have told you his name. By the way, they'll come a time when I may not be able to discuss some things with you."

"You tell us everything or we let Grams run the show."

Kal looked like he'd chugged vinegar. "I'll share everything short of jeopardizing a conviction. But don't tell Grams anything. No offense but she's a loose cannon."

I smacked my palm against my forehead. "We can't hold out on Grams! She'd never forgive us. Leave it to us, we'll keep her under control."

Kal smiled at WonderDog and Puff as they cuddled together. He patted his jacket pocket. "I'll get this soap to the lab. Match or not you'll know when I know. One more thing, do not go after Rex Marchmain or his son. I'll handle it."

I walked him to the door.

"I'm glad you told me about the Masked Dangler. Now stay out of this case—you're all too emotionally involved."

I smiled. "Of course we will."

I returned to the living room and plopped onto the sofa where

Kal had been sitting. The seat was still warm. Warm butt—warm heart?

"I have a question." Lizzy crossed her arms over her chest. "Is there anything between you and Kal?"

"A little friction, some competition, and a friendship." I squinted at her. "We have a business to build. I'm not losing my focus."

"Just asking. It's not that I have any feelings for him. I just don't want to see him get hurt." She nibbled on her thumb. "My father hurt him enough when he broke us up—he went out of his way to say nasty things about Kal's family. He did it in front of me. Nelson Dingler—Masked Dangler—Rotten Egg."

I chuckled. "Rotten egg? That's the worst insult you can think of?"

Lizzy shrugged. "I have this idea dancing in my head. We need to spend some quiet time at my father's apartment. Just feeling the vibes. We might get a clue that way."

"That's not a bad idea. I wasn't thinking clearly when we there right after those forensic bozos made such a mess."

"Grams is going to insist on coming."

"Of course. Besides, she has the key," I said. "How about I pick you, Grams, and Pam up before the shop opens? I can come by at seven tomorrow morning." Parallel parking stood in a dark corner of my mind.

WonderDog jumped to attention as Lizzy grabbed her purse. He slurped Puff, his wide tongue covering most of her back.

"That was some goodbye kiss!"

I bent and scooped up my little fur ball. Together we walked Lizzy and WonderDog to the door. "See you tomorrow. Be ready to leave when I pull up."

"Aren't I always ready on time?"

I snorted.

She giggled.

A strong night breeze swept in as I closed the door behind her. Ivy's note blew from the foyer table to the floor.

With a sigh I unfolded it.

> *We must meet to talk about the shop.*
> *I'll see you tomorrow morning!*
> *Ivy*

CHAPTER 19

*P*uff's breath tickled my ear while the sound of the waves sweeping the shore announced morning's arrival. The clock read six. Just enough time for a quick shower, no hair washing, and out the door.

Cats love routine. Same time. Same steps. From the ear-breathing to the feeding to my dressing with her help, Puff had us on a schedule. After she'd marched me through our program, I kissed the top of her head, grabbed my tote and dashed out the door.

The drive to Lizzy's took me exactly ten minutes. Grams, Pam, Lizzy and WonderDog stood on the front porch. You could have knocked me over with a finch feather. Lizzy on time!

Grams was very grumpy.

Lizzy silently mouthed, "I told her about Kal."

Oookaay. I'd stay away from any subject vaguely related to Kal.

"I'm driving," Grams said, hoisting her pink trousers high up on her middle. She nodded to the Edsel.

Please no windshield notes.

Lizzy rode shotgun while Pam, WonderDog, and I piled into the backseat. The Edsel still had room for a basketball team.

Grams turned the key and the car's bad muffler gave out a hotrod roar. We bounced along the quiet Starfish Cove streets feeling every pothole. WonderDog gave me an apologetic lick on the cheek each time he fell into my lap.

Nelson's building was in the business section of Old Town. Three short blocks of mostly office buildings with retail shops. A tad after seven a.m. it was too early for any street parking challenges.

Grams glanced in her side mirror, turned the hula-hoop wheel twice, and the monster mobile was tucked neatly six inches from the curb.

Grams' gang plus WonderDog made for a tight fit in the elevator. We rode up in the little box in silence.

"Ignore the yellow crime tape," Grams said. "It's only there to keep out the riffraff." She ferretted the apartment key from her purse. It turned in the lock with a soft click.

We walked into a dust cloud—a fiesta of fingerprint powder. Someone left on the overhead fans multiplying the particles.

I secured the door behind us and muffled a cough. We tiptoed into the dining room—the scene of Dingler's last dangle. WonderDog sniffed the rug and sneezed.

"Why are we sneaking?" Grams said. "I can do what I want and what I want is to sit here and close my eyes."

She plopped down on the sofa—causing an eruption of powder — facing the open plan dining area and the killer chandelier. "I'm going to be concentrating so don't talk. Just hush!" With that she shut her eyes.

Lizzy, Pam, and I exchanged shrugs. We each took an armchair —causing similar eruptions—settled in, and closed our eyes. I peeked once and saw WonderDog standing alert but with his eyes closed too.

Come on vibes! I kept my eyes shut and my lips taut in my thinking mode. Was the killer—or killers— waiting for Dingler when he came home or did he let them in?

Grams began to cough. The hacking wracked her tiny body lifting her up from her seat and plunking her down, raising even more powder. She began to gasp.

Pam jumped up. "Grams can't take this dust."

"Does that go to the roof garden?" I pointed at an L-shaped staircase that led to a landing and a door about twenty feet above our heads.

"Nelson's rose garden." Grams said between coughs. "Let's get some fresh air."

Pam helped Grams up the staircase. Lizzy, WonderDog, and I followed.

Grams threw the deadbolt and we stepped through the door into a charming garden—the perfect spot for us to collect our thoughts and breathe. A huge potted ficus tree shaded a cast iron patio table with six matching chairs.

Pam tried to help Grams into one of the chairs. She shook her head. "I got it. Not helpless yet."

It didn't take Grams long to clear her coughing. "Lizzy and Olive, you better sit before Pam tries to make like a nurse with you too."

Pam rolled her eyes. Grams rolled her eyes. We all sat.

A chest-high stone wall extended around the entire roof leaving no way to access the garden except through the apartment. Neighbors in the slightly taller buildings might see through the shrubbery, but this time of day the offices should all be empty.

To my left was a patch of deep red American Beauties— bordered by low rising pink cabbage roses while tea roses in a muted shade of brown worked their way up a nearby trellis. Tucked under a cloak of ivy stood a small white gardener's shed.

Perhaps tending roses gave Nelson a sense of touching beauty in his otherwise ugly world? The image of him lugging his gardening tools, a straw hat on his head, and a bucket in his hands passed through my mind.

From what I could see the rose petals were curling at the edges. A pity no one was tending them.

A deep cleansing breath—out with the bad conclusions, in with the good. Who was most likely to have murdered Nelson Dingler? The man led a dark life leaving a lot of damaged people in his wake.

The soap was the signature of someone who knew his secret identity and had seen him perform. The killer knew he'd try to grab the rope made slippery by the soap.

Grams fluttered her hand to catch my attention. "All that coughing shook an idea loose. The *Silverfish Gazette* challenge was a threat that might expose the Masked Dangler's identity—and maybe Silas' cold case, too."

She cracked her knuckles again. I wished she'd stop doing that.

"I'm thinking it was all set to go down at the Magicians' Fusion," Grams said. "Whoever is really behind this will be there—probably performing."

Her gaze flitted from me to Lizzy to Pam. "It's going to be dangerous. But if Lizzy and Olive keep their heads, we'll all be fine."

CHAPTER 20

f we keep our heads?

"Here's my plan," Grams said. "Olive and Lizzy, you'll go undercover as magicians' assistants ready to perform in the Fusion on April Fools' Day. Magicians love to impress the ladies. Someone is bound to take a shine to you gals and let secrets slip out. All we need to know is if there was someone else besides that half-wit Whodunit involved in challenging Nelson and if so why?"

Wow! If that was a plan, I was an aardvark. But I wasn't going to deny Grams no matter how wild the goose chase got. Maybe her crazy scheme would pay off. Stranger things have happened...maybe.

"Olive, do you have any tricks up your sleeves?" Lizzy said, a mischievous smile playing around the corners of her mouth.

I shook my head. The only mystic stuff I knew had to do with Nonna's magical cold cream.

"You don't have to know anything about magic," Grams said. "They'll hire you as window dressing. Pretty assistants are the real secret to magic. While all eyes are on you, the magician pulls the rabbit from his jacket."

"It could be fun." I said. "As long as we don't have to wear skimpy costumes—I prefer slacks and a blouse—dressy casual."

Pam chuckled. "Dressy casual will really pack the house. You've got to show some thigh or at least some glitz."

"I can assure you these thighs have not been exposed except on the beach."

"There was that time at the Billow's Hotel—you wore a bathing suit then," Lizzy reminded me.

"That turned out real well. I almost drowned." I looked at the Dingler ladies. "No thighs."

Lizzy gathered her hair in two hands, piled it on her head, and held it there with one hand. She puffed out her chest. "I could pull it off."

"You won't need costumes or thighs," Grams said. "Lizzy, some of your jumpsuits are pretty flashy—no offense, dear. They're not racy but they're definitely glitzy. You and Olive are about the same size—you'll work it out."

I was warming to the idea. Or maybe I was trying to convince myself that for Grams' sake, it wasn't as harebrained as I thought. However, our lack of hocus-pocus knowledge might be dangerous. My personal liability insurance didn't cover strapping someone into a straightjacket and sinking them in a dunk tank. Could we find the killer before anyone got hurt including us?

"Why not Pam, too?" Lizzy asked.

"Because your sister's a phobic fibber and besides she's built like me—low to the ground. You and Olive aren't tall but you're not shorties either. Much better stage presence," Grams said. "Besides I need Pam's muscles with me."

"I must tell Kal—just in case." I said.

"Heck no!" Grams grumbled. "Bad enough you and Lizzy

already blabbed to him. You can handle this. You've investigated before. Just avoid knife throwers or being shot from a cannon—"

"A cannon!" Lizzy and I yelped simultaneously.

Our cry was followed by the sound of breaking glass downstairs in Nelson's apartment.

"Who?" I barely got the word out before WonderDog jumped into action. He ran like his tail was on fire, taking the stairs at a gallop.

Nurses really *are* fast on their feet—Pam ran two steps ahead of me.

Lizzy and Grams brought up the rear.

We clambered down the stairs and into the apartment.

A woman dressed in a pale blue caftan with a gold chain around her neck stood in the open space between the living room and dining room. She flashed a laser-white smile at us.

The intruder had dark eyes, longish brunette hair, and a pleasant expression. There was an aura of calm about her. It was as if our collective adrenalin had run into a pillow.

Lizzy gasped.

"I'm sorry if I frightened you." The lady in blue pointed to the pieces of a crystal vase that lay on the floor. "I heard a yell and turned around too fast. My sleeve caught the budvase."

She extended her hand first to Pam and then to Lizzy. "It's a joy to see you!"

The Dingler sisters each took a step back. Neither one spoke. The tension in the air crackled.

"Irma? What the deuce are you doing here?" Grams said, hands on her hips, black orthopedic shoes covered in dust. She didn't make a move towards the woman, who seemed to withdraw from Grams' angry glare.

"This is Irma, my father's most recent ex-wife," Lizzy said to me. "I'm sorry. I don't know what last name you're using. Are you still a Dingler?"

The brunette smiled. "As the new leader of the Seven Planets I'm known only as *The Irma*—but you can call me Irma."

"Who's the dude on the floor?" Grams pointed to a man in a matching caftan and long blond hair, sitting cross-legged under the chandelier. The guy was spinning seven ping pong-sized balls each mounted on a spindle. Chanting something unintelligible, he didn't look up and managed to ignore WonderDog's efforts to grab the balls.

"He's my assistant—my strength, Cosmos. We came immediately when I read about Nelson. It was the least I could do."

Grams grunted at the irony.

"We're Cosmic Travelers here to send Nelson's celestial being to Trappist-1, our mother planet. It's what he would have wanted." She steepled her hands and bowed her head.

I witnessed Nelson's hissy fit when he discovered Irma took all his possessions and ran off to join a cult. What he would have wanted from her was something a bit more retaliatory rather than a spirit sendoff.

WonderDog jumped as Grams growled. "You're not sending Nelson anywhere! My poor son is in the morgue. Now get your cultish butt out of here!" She advanced on Irma, her tiny fists clenched.

The woman in blue maintained her tranquil air as she appealed to Lizzy. "We're running late—a celestial transition should ideally be done at sunrise. We hit traffic on the Turnpike and it delayed our arrival. Cosmos and I need only one thing, one item of Nelson's—and we can complete his journey."

"You've got his Remington painting. Use that!" Lizzy snapped.

I'd never witnessed Lizzy's anger before. The worst thing she'd done was to call her father a rotten egg. Her bubbly persona morphed into a heated boil. The smile gone from her face, her eyes glowed like those of a tiger. "You robbed my father of some of his dearest possessions! Just get out of here and take what's his name with you!" Her nostrils flared. "You have a lot of nerve!"

Lizzy's bottled up emotions came spewing out—all the hurt she felt over losing her father now became Irma's fault. It was bound to happen. A distraction was needed before they came to blows.

It was time for me to roll up my family therapist sleeves. Never one to belittle a person's beliefs I phrased my distraction question as kindly as I could. "What kind of crazy cult are you running?"

CHAPTER 21

There was serenity in Irma's eyes even as she nervously fiddled with the charms on the chain around her neck. Her reply was slow in coming. "Take my words to heart. The Seven Planets is hardly *crazy*. Someday earth will no longer be habitable. We are preparing to transition. The planet Trappist-1 is only thirty-nine light years away. Think of it—our next home is within touching distance."

She raised an index finger pointing to the ceiling. "Seven planets circle Trappist-1, a star in the Aquarius Constellation. They're the size of the earth or smaller. The third planet is capable of sustaining life and celestial spirits. We've started with the spirits first—sending them to that planet which we call Karma."

I felt a charley horse in my left eyebrow.

"We transport celestial beings everyday. Within a few years we'll begin our own pre-celestial journey—uniting families with those who have gone before."

"This is bull-puppies!" Grams elbowed past me, coming nose to neck with Irma. "Get out of my sight and take the guy with the balls with you. Pronto!"

Irma drew herself up to her full height. She had two inches on me. "I have every right to be here. I'm still married to Nelson Dingler—he never served the final papers on me." She took a deep satisfied breath.

"That's because he couldn't find you!" Grams snarled.

"Legally, you have no right to my father's possessions including his celestial being." Pam spoke in a controlled tone made all the more menacing by the softness of her voice.

Irma nodded a benign smile gracing her face.

"Before you leave," I put a hand on the cultist's shoulder. "How did you get in here? I locked the door behind us."

"The door was open—ajar as a matter of fact." Irma motioned to Cosmos to stand. He stopped his spinning balls, pulled a white cloth bag from under the hem of his caftan and carefully placed each ball in the bag.

"We'll be back!" She snapped her fingers. Cosmos rose and floated after her as she exited the apartment.

I closed and locked the door behind them.

"What do you think, Grams?" Lizzy said.

"She read about Nelson's passing and swooped in for a second haul," Grams eyes were cold, flinty. "But what's with the guy with the balls? My son would have a stroke if he knew Irma was messing with his celestial being!" She knotted her face. "Whatever that is."

It sounds like she believes that mumbo-jumbo she spouted. I've read about the star Trappist-1 and the possibility that one of its planets is earthlike."

"*The Irma*," Lizzy corrected.

I checked my watch. "Geez! It's eight-forty-five. Grams can you drop Lizzy and me off at the shop?"

"Let's be sure Irma's left the building," Pam said. She tiptoed out into the small lobby and zipped back in. "The elevator light reads G. They must be on the ground floor. Looks like they left."

"Lizzy you take the bedrooms. Pam and Grams can you secure the garden door? I'll check the other rooms," I said. "Let's be sure we're not locking any cultists in the apartment. Watch out for the broken glass. No time to clean up."

Kal was bound to spot the fragments.

Lizzy and I exchanged the all-clear sign by yelling, "All clear!"

The Dinglers, WonderDog, and I left the apartment, adjusting the yellow tape. It drooped on one side—blame it on the humidity.

Grams locked the apartment door. "You test it Olive."

I jiggled the knob, then pushed and pulled. "Locked."

We were off to the shop. Cutting it close. Late opening again.

I hoped nobody was waiting for us.

CHAPTER 22

"*N*o..." I groaned as Grams slid the Edsel into our parking lot.

A sleek black sedan sat close to the entrance right under the sign that read *Nonna's Cold Cream.* The lights were on in the shop and the window display was illuminated.

"I didn't hit anything," Grams said. "What're you whining about?"

"That's Myron car. The shop is open. Ivy still has the key. I'm not ready to deal with her—them!"

Grams kept the engine running. "Out you go. I've no time for Ivy's know-it-alls and Myron's *Godfather* routine. Pam and I are going to the Yacht Club for brunch and snooping."

"Have fun. Wish I could go with you." She had no idea how much I wished it. I stepped reluctantly from the car.

"Just apply your psychology," Lizzy said. "You're good at tough love. I'll be right behind you."

WonderDog leapt out of the car, ears and tail erect sensing our tension.

"Remember your assignment!" Grams called. "After work get

over to the arena in your snazziest jumpsuits and theatrical makeup. Don't come back until they hire you."

Thinking of that didn't help the Ivy-induced knot in my stomach. Before I could evict Ivy from our business I had to lather a description of the soap buyer from her. Also, there was Myron's nose to consider—he had a snoot for crime.

The bell over the door jangled as Lizzy, WonderDog, and I walked into the shop. It was *our* place and yet I felt prickly all over —as if wearing a linen dress.

"You're late!" The crumpled tissue paper voice came from behind the counter.

My jaw locked—probably a good thing as it kept my tongue in place.

Myron and Ivy stood side-by-side—the sight of them was enough to turn away our most devoted cold cream customers. They looked like Starfish Cove's version of American Gothic sans pitchfork.

"If we're going to make changes—and we need to make changes —then you gals have to put in the hours!" Ivy said, tapping her fingers on the countertop. Her hands resembled a pawnshop window with rings on all of ten of her fingers.

I ground my teeth so hard I thought I'd cracked a molar.

Other than a nod, Myron didn't greet us. I could see what side of the bed his bread was buttered on. He was helping Ivy move in on our territory. I gave the anxiety-ridden mobster the best counseling money could buy and this was the thanks I got.

Lizzy kept a doggy bed near the front windows. WonderDog circled the mat twice and then settled in for a snooze, evidently exhausted by our tension.

"Let's get to work—" Ivy took a notebook from Myron and plunked it on the counter.

Bad news is best served with an appetizer of compliments. "You've been a wonderful help, Ivy. We do appreciate your efforts.

Let's visit the backroom. Show me what supplies we need." Privacy was required in order to retire Ivy from *Nonna's Cold Cream* with her dignity intact.

Lizzy directed her charm to Myron. "So tell me what you've been up to? I'll bet the ladies who lunch in Manhattan are missing you." She twirled her hair and licked her lip. Being a typical male Myron fell into the trap—they all do.

Ivy and I slipped behind the curtain. I escorted her to the far side of the room to avoid being overheard. Before I alienated her I needed to pluck a description of the soap buyer from her little gray cells.

"This is where our stock of lavender soap was." I pointed to the spot on the floor where the two cartons of forty-eight bars of soap had been. "It's great that you sold them all but tell me a bit about the buyer. Just curious."

"Let's talk about my ideas. With my experience we could save this little shop and make it a success."

Ivy's suggestion that we weren't doing well stung. The cold cream business was our baby and it was growing at a nice pace. We didn't need her Manhattan Macy's ideas. The shop was mom and pop or in this case Olive and Lizzy. Period.

Instead of responding I redirected. "Can you recall what the soap buyer looked like?"

"Of course I remember. Macy's trained us to retain details in case we were ever robbed. I mean…he wasn't a robber. He paid. But here you go."

She began to count off on the fingers of her left hand. "Build— slight, your height. Race—white. Age—not more than thirty. Hair —shaved head. Eyes—bluish-green. I've run out of fingers but I'll keep on going."

I sighed a noisy gust of air.

Ivy looked over my shoulder as if the guy was standing behind me. "He had full lips. I've always thought that kind of girly for a man. I can't say there was anything fishy about him—I mean he didn't smell fishy. Most folks around Starfish Cove have a sea breeze-fish odor. So he wasn't local."

I bent my head taking a whiff of me. I hadn't thought about that before. The sea breeze odor wasn't offensive and at times it mingled with suntan oil and gave off a pleasant piña colada aroma. But I still sniffed. I didn't smell fishy but I still detected a trace of Eau de WonderDog.

"He was wearing a blue and white striped polo shirt, baggy white trousers and those leather slip-on shoes they wear on boats."

"Did he have an accent?"

"He just sounded cheerful. Like I told you the soap was for his sister's wedding shower. Asked where he could get ribbon and empty goodie bags."

"Besides being cheerful was there anything else about his behavior?"

"He acted nervous like he was rushed. Got the soap, paid, and then carried the cartons out to his car. I offered to help but he said no."

Imagine that, a young healthy guy refusing help from an octogenarian. He seemed normal enough. He liked our distinctive soap that contained hand-crushed lavender blooms. The question that niggled at me was how a non-local male happened into our little shop.

"Let's get on to business," Ivy said. "Every morning we had department meetings at Macy's. We need to start doing that."

"About Macys." I took a deep breath and reached into my bag of tricks for disappointing people without hurting them. "Ivy, we really appreciate all the thought you've given to our shop."

"But...?" Her dark eyes flashed. "I hear a *but* coming."

No matter what I said this was going to end badly. "Part of the joy of starting a new business is learning from your mistakes. It's about having a partner who can take up where you're weak and vice-versa. Lizzy could sell the Sunshine Skyway Bridge to camel drivers in the Sahara. I'm not a salesperson, but I have business sense and training in understanding human nature."

Ivy's bottom lip popped out like a Pez dispenser.

"It's not to say your ideas don't have value, because they do—you do. But Lizzy and I are special friends and confidants as well as partners. Very often a partnership works with two people but not three. From the beginning we agreed to take this journey alone —together."

"I understand." She threw her head back and dashed from the room.

One step behind her I watched as she flung herself against Myron. He wrapped his arms around her, his heavy gold cufflinks locking together. He jiggled and yanked unable to free his wrists. Ivy was locked in his arms.

"May I?" I approached despite his look to kill. "Hold still."

The corner of one cufflink was hung on the other. I jiggled them free. He released Ivy and she stood back sniffling. She was a woman used to getting her way. Sometimes the more you get to know someone, the less you wish you did.

Lizzy shot me a *now what* look. I gave her a slight shake of my head.

Careful not to utter anything that would give Ivy or Myron encouragement I said, "We treasure your friendship—both of you. But we just can't add a third partner." I didn't add, "Especially one who comes with a pet mobster."

Myron dropped his voice to noir. "You might want to consider taking out insurance on your little shop."

"After all we've been through, you'd strong arm me?" I said.

He blushed. "You're right. You're right!" He threw his arms in the air. There's no reason this should get out of hand. You'll always be my little shiksa but now I've got a responsibility to Ivy. There's only one thing left to do."

I braced myself, clenching my fists. All the time I gave Myron putting his anxiety attacks before all my needs—even canceling trips to see Nonna—didn't count for diddly. He wanted to impress his lady friend. I waited to hear what he had in mind.

"Ivy wants a cosmetic shop. I'm gonna set her up in business. There's a fancier, bigger store for rent up the boulevard. I'll sign the lease and she can sell her own goop for dames."

That was a catchy name. *Goop for Dames.*

He gave me a wink. I took it as a token of friendship unbroken. "Sorry Olive. You just got yourself some competition," he said.

Ivy grabbed her purse from under the counter and they strutted out the door.

CHAPTER 23

"*W*ell that went well!" Lizzy said, a dimple nipping at the corner of her mouth.

"A little competition is good for business." I felt the burden lift from my shoulders. The suspense was over. The deed was done. The only *we* at *Nonna's Cold Cream* would be Lizzy and me.

"I just lost a good babysitter," Lizzy said. "And Heather lost her poker-playing coach."

"It'll sort itself out. Ivy's just feeling rejected right now. She'll forgive us." I scanned the shop. "Let's put everything the way it was before Ivy created a mini-Macys."

I rubbed my brow, it cramped again. "I forgot to ask her for the key! Just as well. It's easier to get the locks changed."

"Call locksmith." I spoke into my cell and the phone fairy responded with the names of three local experts. One call and a locksmith was on his way.

"We're still out of lavender soap and getting no place fast." Nervous energy coursed through my body.

I caught sight of a brown car pulling into the lot. Whoever it was parked alongside the shop and out of my view.

"Customer!" I alerted Lizzy.

WonderDog stood at attention his tail wagging.

We were both behind the counter when *The Irma* walked in. Her hair was perfectly coifed like Princess Leia in *Star Wars* and her teeth shined like car headlights. She wore her light blue cult caftan and gold chain with a couple of tiny trinkets hanging from it.

"Lizzy, dear! I've come to see your little shop!" She floated from the door to the counter. I couldn't see if her feet were actually touching the floor but the illusion confuzzled me.

Lizzy tensed.

"I read all about your opening in the *Silverfish Gazette* and would have come earlier but the Seven Planets had me spinning. I'm truly thrilled for you both."

There was something tender about the woman. She emanated serenity put with an underlying pathos. WonderDog trotted to her side looking at her adoringly.

"Lizzy, your father would be so proud of you."

"I seriously doubt that. He barely acknowledged my existence."

"Dearest, I know he came across cold as ice, but he did love you and Pam. He just couldn't show it." She reached across the counter catching Lizzy's hand. "There was a time when I was intensely jealous of you, but now all I feel is love." She rubbed her thumb and index finger over the charms on her gold chain.

If it was an act, it was well done. I discovered I'd been holding my breath, and let it out softly.

"You were jealous of me?" Lizzy's eyes widened.

"He boasted about you constantly. When you started *List with Lizzy* he mocked me and said I'd never have the nerve to start my own business. He said you took after him."

Lizzy gripped the sides of her head as if to cover her ears. "That's not true. He never said a kind word to me." She looked at me as if I held the answer.

I felt an ache in my throat. "Perhaps your father did care about you. Lots of people are incapable of showing their feelings. They keep everything bottled inside. I'm sorry you had to learn this way but it's good for you to know."

"I had no idea." Lizzy brushed a hand against her cheek.

The bell jingled and two ladies walked into the shop laughing uproariously. One had skin as pale as mine and the other had a lovely cocoa-colored complexion. They wore their hair in almost identical curly bobs.

"I'll take care of them," I said.

Lizzy shook her head. "I'd rather. I don't need to think about my father right now." She slipped past me and greeted the women putting on her bubbly smile like a secret weapon. "Welcome to Nonna's Cold Cream! How can I help you?"

I turned to Irma, her face lit in a kindly smile. "It's the truth. Nelson talked incessantly about Lizzy—sometimes Pam—but always Lizzy this and Lizzy that. He was a hard man, but he did love her."

She reached over and patted my hand. "You're a good friend for Lizzy. I can see you give her the confidence Nelson took from her. She may still hold anger in her heart toward me and I don't fault her for that. But beneath her anger I sense a new happiness. I know the universe will bless your business and it will succeed. I wanted you to know that before I left."

"I'm curious about the charms on your chain. Can you share their meanings?"

Irma lifted the chain separating the gold pieces. "This circle represents Trappist-1." She slid it aside and held the next ornament—seven small circles linked together—the blue one represents the planet Karma. And this little key unlocks my opportunity to journey there."

"They're very pretty. I'm sure they keep you from feeling home sick."

"Cosmos and I are returning to our community tomorrow—before we leave we may try once more to send Nelson's celestial being on its journey—I hate to fail my mission."

"You truly believe in your Seven Planets?" I felt a release of my tension as I stared into her eyes.

"Of course. I wouldn't have taken all of Nelson's possessions if I didn't. I planned on leaving him anyway but his earthly goods made my ascendancy possible. Materialistic, cruel, and mean, he deserved to lose everything in support of the Seven Planets."

She looked down at WonderDog. He hadn't moved from her side. Irma ran her hand from the top of his head to under his chin. "Go to your bed."

The hound blinked once and returned to his bed. He lay down, placed his head over his paws and closed his eyes.

My liking for Irma was happening too quickly. The woman was an admitted thief and surely a con artist with her celestial being transportation system. Had she hypnotized me? I didn't believe that person could instantly control an unwilling subject, but I'd never met a person as ethereal as Irma. I pinched my left arm as hard as I could, but I still felt a fondness for her.

"The only thing Nelson cared about were material possessions and that Remington painting. Do you know he cheated a little old Appalachian lady out of it? He traded her three velvet art paintings —those creations that were the rage in the 60s."

Dingler was a real slime ball.

"I am not proud of what I did," Irma said, "but everything he owned he got by cheating. He deserved to lose it all. It went to a good cause. I have mastered many talents since leaving his control —talents beyond what even a doctor of the mind such as yourself might imagine. I have my freedom. I have my power."

"Where is the Remington now?"

"I finally found a buyer willing to pay its appraised value plus pay for a guaranteed position on the first moon of Trappist-1. He took delivery last week. The painting is gone and with it the last of Nelson Dingler—except for his celestial being."

She winked. "I wished I was a fly on the wall when he returned from his golf game and found the apartment empty except for a single cot!" Her eyes twinkled with mischief. "That cot held special significance for us."

"Excuse me for a minute. Lizzy needs my help." I tore myself away and stepped to Lizzy's side. One hundred and one uses for a single cot taunting me.

The two customers continued their cheerful cacophony as we tallied their bills. The women seemed to have the kind of friendship Lizzy and I shared. No words were necessary to kick in giggle fits. Their laughter was contagious and soon the four of us were yucking it up over nothing.

I packaged their cold creams, under-eye creams and lotions, wrapping them carefully in tissue and slipping them into two logoed bags.

The more we tried to stop laughing the harder we laughed. The pointless giggling was a much-needed release for Lizzy. All her bottled-up emotions came pouring out in snorts and chuckles.

"Please hurry back," I said, handing the women their bags. "And bring your laughter with you. You made our day!"

We returned to Irma. I was unable to wipe the smile from my face.

"It's good to see you both laughing. It's a healing thing. If you'd like to learn more about my Seven Planets here's my number." She placed a light blue business card on the counter. A picture of what must be Trappist-1 with seven dots circling it was stamped above *THE IRMA* with a phone number below it.

"If you need to talk to us or feel the need for counseling, here's our card." I handed her one of our Nonna's Cold Cream cards.

She took the card, slipped it in the pocket of her caftan, then raised her left hand in some sort of salute. "May the Seven Planets guide you!"

The Irma glided out the door bumping into the locksmith.

I recognized him by the word *Locksmith* stitched on his shirt pocket. In less than ten minutes the jolly fellow with the Spanish accent changed the locks on the front and back door. He gave me three keys and a bill—slid my credit card through his little gizmo and was out the door.

Lizzy and I now had fresh keys with one to spare. It was a relief to know I didn't have to ask Ivy to return the key. She should have offered and perhaps someday she would. Meantime our shop was secured.

CHAPTER 24

"Almost three," I said. "Time to become glittery magician assistants. I'm excited about the new experience of sleuthing in disguise. We'll need professional names—maybe Belle and Star?"

Lizzy chuckled. "I've always been fond of the name Bree. How about Bree and Dee?"

"Okay—Bree and Dee. Let's shut down."

She clicked off the counter lights. "Thank goodness for those last customers. It would have been a lean day without them."

I tucked away the displays. "Replacement mirrors should be delivered tomorrow. I hope the thief enjoys the ones he stole." I shut down the rest of the lights.

My phone pinged. "It's a text message from Kal. The soap on the rope matches our lavender soap. He wants to see us."

Lizzy and I traded shrugs.

"Meeting with Kal isn't going to change anything. It is what it is. Someone is trying to frame us." I said.

"We made a promise to Grams. I'd rather deal with an angry

cop than my ticked-off grandmother," Lizzy said. "Let's go break into show business."

"If I don't respond he'll track us down—might even blunder into the arena and blow our cover." I drafted a response text. "Can't meet tonight—something personal came up. Unavoidable. Will connect in the morning. Not to worry."

Lizzy took my phone, read the message, and handed it back. "That will drive him bonkers but it should hold him until tomorrow."

WonderDog knew it was time to leave—he joined us at the front door. While Lizzy locked up, he galloped down the stairs and ran to the fire hydrant at the corner of the lot. He gave it a good watering and then trotted back to where we stood staring numbly at the empty parking area.

"Nuts!" Lizzy said. "I forgot Grams brought us. Our cars are at my house."

Faster than I could say *Uber* Jaimie cruised into the parking lot in her yellow convertible. Good news—a ride. Bad news—a ride with whip lips. We'd have to shake her before we donned our glittery disguises. It was impossible for her to keep a secret.

"Poshookly!" Jaimie said. "I'm headed out to Joe's on the Beach. Thought I'd kidnap you gals. It's been ages since we had a girls' night out."

There are some people you remain friends with for reasons you can't explain—Jaimie Toast was that kind of friend. At times so outrageously funny she'd have Lizzy and me in tears and other times so mean-mouthed I wished for duct tape. But without Lizzy and me, she'd crumble to dust and blow away. We didn't have the heart to let that happen.

"Great timing. We're without wheels," I said making a thumbing-a-ride motion.

"Jump in! Joe's on the Beach here we come!"

Neither Lizzy nor I commented as we walked to Jaimie's

convertible. I slipped in the front seat, and put my tote bag between my feet. Lizzy and WonderDog clambered in the back.

"My place, please?" Lizzy said. She rested her head against the seat, donned her Audrey Hepburn sunglasses, and basked in the sun.

Jaimie said something about Joe's but I pretended not to hear.

We cruised up the boulevard looking like a Chamber of Commerce promo for Starfish Cove—a bright yellow convertible carrying two blondes, a honey brown, and a Brillo-haired hound. Okay—except for the Brillo-haired hound.

Thankfully the wind made too much noise to converse. The seven-minute drive didn't allow much time to think of a reason why Jaimie couldn't come with us. She was bound to ask—insist.

Jaimie brought her car to a screeching halt in Lizzy's driveway. "You gals never answered. Is Joe's okay or would you prefer the Tradewinds?"

"Tonight's not a good night." I closed the car door. "We have unchangeable plans. How about next Thursday? I'll be the designated driver."

"Why not today? What's going on that we can't do together?"

"We're going to a costume dinner." Lizzy feigned disappointment. "I wish you could join us but it's by invitation only."

Jaimie had parked in the driveway behind our cars, boxing us in. We were stuck with her at least for the time being—harmless enough if she didn't catch on to our scheme.

"Curfoop!" She said. "I was looking forward to raising a little lamboutle with my two besties!"

The *Loud Mouth of the South* had her own language, nonsense words that often brought us to giggles. Her oddball language was the signature of a brilliant but directionless mind. It would be fascinating to delve into the dark corners of her noggin but I feared if I got in, I'd never get out.

"Can I see your costumes?" Jaimie linked her arm in mine and marched up the stairs.

WonderDog watered the daisy patch by the front steps while Lizzy unlocked the door.

The finches fluttered, rearranged themselves, and chirped merrily as we all entered.

Jaimie plopped down on the sofa, stuck out one finger, and invited a bird. One landed on her knuckle and another on her head. Lizzy stood behind her making throat-cutting motions directed at me. We needed to lose Jaimie but if she sensed an adventure in the works she'd stick to us like beach tar.

"My little birds need their seed cups filled," Lizzy said. "Olive, can you take care of WonderDog? His kibble is on the bottom shelf of the pantry."

"Watching you two feed the livestock is not my idea of fun. I'm thirsty." Jaimie strode to the wet bar, pulled a bottle of vodka from the small refrigerator, along with a lime which she sliced with the speed and flair of a professional bartender. By the time I'd opened the kibble, she downed her drink and was going for a second.

I filled WonderDog's dish and then quickly took the bottle from Jaimie. With a firm grip on her upper arm I escorted her back to the sofa. "You're driving. If you even sniff another glass I'm calling Kal."

She crossed her arms and sunk onto the sofa. "Fine!"

"WonderDog!" Lizzy called. She pointed at Jaimie. "She sits! You watch!"

The dog stood at Jaimie's feet pinning her with his eyes.

"We'll be trying on outfits in the bedroom. It'll take a few minutes." Lizzy said, motioning me toward her room. "Talk about bad timing," she mumbled, closing the door behind us. "I love her to death—most of the time—but she really needs a new hobby."

Lizzy pushed open the mirrored door to her walk-in closet. A good fifteen feet deep it was Charlie's Angels, Mary Quant, and a touch of Twiggy—a step back in time.

"The dressier outfits are back here." She ran her hand over the rack.

"You have an impressive collection of retro duds."

"I get them at vintage clothing boutiques. The local consignment shops know to call me when anything from the sixties or seventies comes in."

She pulled out a silver jumpsuit with a wide metallic belt and big black enamel buckle. "How about this for you?"

I burst into laughter. "What possessed you to buy that thing? It looks like a fireman's suit or something from outer space."

"Truth is, I've never worn it. I might put it on eBay."

"How about this?" The denim jumpsuit she held out looked as if it had been used to train Bedazzlers.

"Please tell me you never wore that."

Lizzy blushed. "I once wore it as a joke to a come as you are party." She tucked it back on the rack.

"I've got it! The perfect costumes." She pulled two jumpsuits holding their hangers one in each hand. Identical in everyway except that one was black and the other white. They had standup collars, wide belts, hidden zippers, with silver studs on the bodice and down their right legs. "I couldn't decide between black or white—so I bought both."

She handed me the black. "The contrast will be great with your blonde hair."

We stripped down to our undies and into the suits. I pulled the zipper on my suit up to a modest spot and buckled the hip-riding belt. I looked at myself in the mirrored closed door. "Why did jumpsuits go out of style? I love the way this looks. I may not give it back."

I turned, admiring my side and rearview. "This takes ten years off."

"Put the zipper down to about here," Lizzy pointed to the spot where she'd left off zipping her white suit. It was a little exposed for my taste but what the heck? No one would know our real names.

"This goes on your belt." Lizzy handed me a tiny purse. "It's to carry your license and cell phone." I clipped it over the hip-rider strap.

"There's no belt on my suit so I'm not bringing my phone." She passed a long red silk scarf to me. "Put it around your neck like this." Demonstrating with a blue scarf, she tucked it under her hair and let the ends hang loose on her chest. "Now fix the collar so it stands up almost touching your ears."

As we stood side-by-side in the mirror our eyes met and we erupted into hysterical giggles. I laughed so hard I couldn't catch my breath—certain that we shared the same thought.

The bedroom door opened. Jaimie and WonderDog stood in the doorway. The hound turned his head right and left as if deciding whether we were in pain. "Is somebody hurt? We heard the ruckus," Jaimie said. "Poshookly! You're going to the costume party dressed as Elvis impersonators!"

My thought—our thoughts exactly. Lizzy and I launched into laughter again.

A case of the hiccups kicked in. When I get them they can linger for hours. Great way to nail a job where silence and composure are important.

The hiccups became more violent, shaking my body. I stood up, clenched my fists, and took a gulp of air.

Lizzy disappeared and reappeared with a full glass of water. "Hold your breath, and drink the whole thing all at once—from the top edge of the glass."

I put the rim of the tumbler to my lips but the water splashed in my face and up my nose. I stopped breathing—my normal reaction to a wet face. Gasping for air I realized I'd ceased hiccupping. The collar of my Elvis suit was soaked and water dribbled down my chest—so much for open zippers.

Lizzy and I cackled like two lunatics while Jaimie wore her self-pitying face, unhappy at being left out. If she couldn't be the center of mirth, she didn't want to play. "Chip just called. We're going to the Don Cesar for a romantic dinner. It will take me hours to get ready. Ciao!"

She waved her car keys, flinging a final zap at us. "You both look very silly!"

Lizzy looked heavenward releasing a deep sigh.

"Time for makeup," I said.

Lizzy motioned me to the kitchen. She placed a Tupperware the size of a file box on the table. It was loaded with intriguing jars, tubes, and compacts of face paint. She centered a lighted makeup mirror and we began the transformation.

"How did you accumulate so much goop?" Not being a saver, her collection astounded me. "You barely wear any makeup."

"I see something in the store, it looks good, it smells yummy, and I buy it. Get it home and I wonder what I could have been thinking. These are mistakes—like my infamous box of glossy lip goop."

"Use these." She handed me a box of clips, combs, and elastics. She bent her head, grabbed her hair with an elastic hairband and fastened it in a lopsided knot on the top of her head.

I imitated my friend and pulled my locks into a silly topknot.

We dove into her collection of paint creating two gals I didn't recognize. I refused false eyelashes but opted for a pencil-drawn cat's eye look. With blush, highlight powder, and contouring shadow Lizzy completely changed the shape of her face. My results were not as successful.

"Let me help you." She took the highlighting brush from my hand. Using a couple of makeup remover pads she wiped off the corpse-like effect I'd taken ten torturous minutes to apply. With a few flicks of highlighter and well-placed strokes of contour shadow she changed my somewhat roundish face into someone even Nonna wouldn't have recognized.

Minutes later two gift-wrapped gals slipped into my car, prepared to talk our way into temporary jobs as magicians' assistants.

WonderDog appeared in the window, his bushy brows crinkled in what had come to be his *what are they up to and why can't I go look?*

CHAPTER 25

*L*izzy and I began our job hunt at the Starfish Cove arena where the Magician's Fusion would take place. Someone there should be able to point us in the direction of the guy in charge of hiring.

I pulled into the employees' parking lot and we hopped out.

Lizzy strutted toward the door marked *private*. She was a natural showgirl—I tried to imitate her. I threw back my shoulders and did a shimmy but it didn't have the same effect.

"Wait up!" I trotted after her. "How do you do that hubba-hubba walk?"

"What are you talking about? The little wiggly thing? I was born that way." She snickered. "You either have it or you don't."

"I've got to add some oomph if I'm going to get hired."

"You'll get hired because I'm not going undercover without you." She put on her thinking face. "Can you pop your hips out? Right and then left and walk as if there are marbles under your feet."

Wiggle-walking couldn't be that hard. I had a PhD from N.Y.U. I focused on the hip thrusts and thought of the imaginary marbles under my shoes. Four steps later it was clear the entire alphabet after my name wouldn't make a spicy walker out of me.

Lizzy shook her head. "You may be hopeless. Wait! I have an idea. Try jazz hands."

"Jazz hands?"

She raised her hands—palms facing me—and moved them back and forth to some unheard rhythm. "Not exactly hootchy-kootchy but it has a certain suggestive energy."

"That is so *not* suggestive. I'll look possessed."

We entered the arena. With a finger raised, Lizzy stopped a guy riding a unicycle. "Where would we find out about employment?"

"The head honcho's office is down that hall. Name's Figgis. A decent enough old codger."

We followed his directions and came to an open door with a sign that read *Manager*.

A chubby fellow sat behind a cluttered desk—he had a barely there comb-over and skin that could use some of Nonna's miracle cream.

"Gotta give you gals credit for trying—you look great in those suits—but we don't need any more Elvis impersonators."

"Are they hiring for the Fusion?"

"The magicians are rehearsing in the staging area. If they don't take you on come back here. I can use you." He winked. "Both."

As we stepped from Figgis' office a muscular guy in a black leotard ran up to us, grabbing my arm. "You gals from the agency?"

Before we could answer he looked us up and down. "Come with me! I'm the one who placed the order. Two of my three assistants walked out this morning. No notice. Not even a goodbye." He grabbed my arm and I grabbed Lizzy—no need to fake our experience.

"I'm the Great Valentine. You can call me V. Let's get you suited up."

"Piece of cake," Lizzy whispered in my ear.

V speed-walked us into a private staging area behind flimsy black drapes.

A ten-foot tall silver missile-thingie dominated the space. Shaped like a ginormous tube of lipstick, three thin black felt-like strips folded into the tube running from the top to the bottom—the center strip wider than the sidepieces. It stood on a chrome platform.

"Your job is to go in the tube and come out alive," He chuckled. "Pay is one hundred bucks each per show. Your costumes are behind the screen. Blondie, you take the glitter dress and fishnet stockings. Wiggles can take the black body suit and fishnets."

The magician stuffed a sheet of paper into Lizzy's hand and another one into mine. "Standard confidentiality agreements. You talk—we squawk."

He handed me a pen. "First *and* last names."

I signed *Marilyn Monroe*—couldn't remember if I was Bree or Dee. Lizzy raised an eyebrow but followed suit signing *Shirley Temple*. We passed them back to V who was shouting orders at a guy carrying a piece of scenery. He grabbed the agreements and the pen, but didn't look at them. The papers disappeared as quickly as they'd appeared.

V was moving way too fast for my comfort. "Does this job have anything to do with cannons or getting cut in half?" I asked.

"Dorrie!" He yelled, ignoring me. "Got the two replacements. Blondie will be the floating head."

A slender dark-haired woman stepped from behind the screen. She wore a sleeveless black bodysuit and fishnet stockings. "In here, girls!"

Did I just agree to lose my head?

"I'm the third dame," Dorrie said, folding the screen around us. "Have you seen the act?"

Lizzy and I shook our noggins.

"Shame. It would help if you had." She flicked her hand at us.

"No matter. You'll catch on." She rummaged through a rolling metal clothes rack, took down a purple sequined shift and a plastic bag containing fishnet stockings. She handed the costume to me.

"Thanks. Sure it'll fit?" I tried to cozy up to her—she might know something we could use.

"The dress fit the last three floating heads and the fishnets stretch—one size fits all." She shrugged. "So far, so good."

I shuddered certain Dorrie hadn't bothered to have the germy costume cleaned.

"How about *that* Masked Dangler challenge?" I asked, hoping it sounded like small talk. The sooner we got the information we came for, the sooner we could skip the costumes and boogie—as Grams would say.

My question struck Dorrie dumb—but only for an instant. "Listen Blondie, we don't talk about the Dangler. He was bad news thirty years ago and it's still considered unlucky to mention his name. We have a saying—*Let sleeping danglers lie*. If you want to last in the business don't bring up his name again."

Dorrie dug out a scrunched up black jersey and held it up—a bodysuit. She ferretted around and pulled out a second pair of tights.

She turned on me. "Take my advice. You're here to work for V. We don't hire groupies or fans of the dark arts. If you're stalking the Masked Dangler—walk now and save me the trouble of training you."

"Geez!" Lizzy hissed. "Magicians!"

"We are not magicians," Dorrie said. "We create illusions that people want to believe. In this case it's done with that big silver cylinder out there. It'll make you look like your body is coming apart."

She cupped my cheeks in her hands. "Blondie, you're *the* face— your head's going to appear to float through the black opening in the center front. This noodle is gonna glide from the top of the tube to bottom and back up again at V's command.

She pointed to Lizzy, "You're the left-side arms and legs. I take the right side."

I cleared my throat. "I'm Olive and this is Lizzy in case you need to identify our bodies."

"Not to worry," Dorrie said. "This is the safest trick in the entire show. V's performed it thousands of times." She handed Lizzy the black body suit and pair of fishnet stockings. "Now hurry up and get dressed!"

We shed our jumpsuits. The air felt chill against my sweaty skin. The fishnet itched my legs but at least the sleeveless A-line dress covered me to my knees. Not about to leave my phone and ID laying about for someone to grab, I fastened the jumpsuit hip belt under the sequined dress—lumpy but passable.

Lizzy shivered as she yanked the fishnet stockings and the sleeveless body suit into place.

Hesitantly we stepped from behind the modesty curtain. V grabbed my hand tugging me past the silver cylinder and to stage right.

Dorrie waved her hand at V. "They need bowing lessons before you tube them."

CHAPTER 26

"They don't know how to bow?" V snarled. "We're not using that agency any more. Dorrie, show them how it's done."

Dorrie strode to where I stood, tugging Lizzy behind her. V's assistant stood between us. "Only Blondie gets to bow in the tube trick."

She pointed to Lizzy. "You and me are never seen. The illusion is her head is floating away from her body. We're Blondie's arms and legs. When V pushes her head down to the floor we stick our hands and gams out the slits near the top—then vice-versa."

"Question?" I raised my hand like a schoolgirl. "Just how is he going to push my head up and down ten feet?"

Dorrie gave me a playful nudge. "It would help to know that, huh?" She waggled her finger leading us behind the giant tube.

"You're not gonna be standing—you'll be laying flat on that." She pointed to a six-foot shelf affixed to the tube at a right angle. "Your head shows through, your body lays flat. The platform is on rollers V operates with his foot. To the audience it looks like he's moving your head but he's just pumping the table up and down."

So simple it was silly.

"How you coming with that bowing?" V called.

"No matter how long we're married he still manages to dish the stress." She stood next to me. "You only get one bow. Just bow from the waist with one hand over your middle. Don't hog the applause. He hates that."

"Run us through the trick one more time." It sounded way too easy.

Dorrie chuckled. "You sure you've worked shows before? You gals couldn't be any greener." She counted off on her fingers. "First V makes a big deal out of the cylinder—the audience ooh's and ah's. Then Blondie walks on stage. He takes your hand. The cylinder opens down the front—as if something split it with a knife from top to bottom. You step in between the two sections paying no attention to me or your friend—I'll be on the left half and she'll be in the right section."

Lizzy and I nodded. So far so good.

"V starts the music and the cylinder closes around you. Quick as a bunny you jump on the hidden shelf and lay flat. Make sure you head sticks out from the minute the cylinder closes. Got it?"

"And I just stick my head out?"

"That's all you have to do—that and smile."

"Do I wave?"

"Geez! No! Your friend and I are your arms and legs. We wave through the splits in the side. You just smile like you're having the time of your life."

I was really glad Kal knew nothing about this—so humiliating.

"V will tap you with his wand when he's ready for the stage-hands to split open the cylinder. When he taps you, get off the shelf like it's on fire. There's a blackout curtain behind you. The only thing the audience will see is you stepping from the cylinder. Whatever you do don't look at your friend or me—we'll be hiding in the sides until it's rolled off stage."

It was almost too simple. Should be illegal to charge people for it.

"The most important thing is the bow. V takes a bunch of bows. Blondie, you take *one* when he points to you. He'll let go of your hand and you leave the stage. He gets all the applause."

"We're ready!" Dorrie called. She paraded us back to V.

Two stagehands opened the tube as if cutting it in half from top to bottom. The right and left sides lay open exposing a dark narrow alcove in each half—the single grooves were more like shadows—the two spaces just large enough to hold a body.

"Get in!" V pointed at Dorrie. "See how she does it? Once the cylinder is upright I'll tap it with my wand. You, Wiggles, you hear the tap, you stick out your right arm and right leg through those black felt lined slits. Just wave. That's all you do."

V grabbed my arm. His touch was cold and clammy. "You get the hard part Blondie." He walked me to the back of the cylinder. "Lay here on your stomach. Poke your head through the cloth." I did as I was instructed, fascinated that this sham actually worked.

"Dorrie, Wiggles, get in your sidecars. Cue the music!"

An eerie tune played from what sounded like a very old CD. I lay on the shelf, arching my neck and readying to poke my head through the felt opening. It was like being in a carwash moving on a conveyor belt.

I heard Lizzy yelp.

"You okay?" I screamed. What were they doing to her?

V slammed his hand over my mouth just before my nose poked through the fabric. "That is your last chance Blondie," he growled. "One more screw up and you're out."

"Just got scared for a minute," Lizzy yelled. "I'm fine!" Her voice sounded muffled.

The germy sweat from V's hand gave me the gags. I wanted to wipe my lips but didn't dare. I closed my eyes and pushed my face through the felt, out the opening as if facing the audience.

When I opened my eyes, I felt like a funhouse skull on a conveyor belt. There was no way I was going to be able to do this in front of a crowd. What if Jaimie just happened to be in the audience? She'd be teasing me until we were both in our graves and beyond.

Just as I slid through the felt strips my cell phone rang at my hip.

V bellowed in anger.

There was just enough time to watch Dorrie pull Lizzy from the tube, before a pair of powerful hands yanked me back through the felt curtain and off the shelf. One of the stagehands had his hammy mitts on me.

"Take your friend and go!" V growled. "I'm calling your agency. You couldn't do worse if you were planted by my competition—not that I have any competition!"

The illusionist turned an odd shade of reddish green, his fists were clenched, and his eyeballs bulged.

Lizzy was waiting for me as I rounded the cylinder, my dignity slightly damaged.

"Gals!" Dorrie called. "Your costumes! I want them back!"

I didn't need to be reminded twice. She was welcome to pass them on to the next floating head and sidekick. We slipped behind the privacy curtain, peeled out of the icky fishnets and into our jumpsuits. Never thought I'd welcome the sight of our Elvis duds.

Infiltrating the magicians' rehearsal was not the best idea. Next time I'd have a *no* handy for any of Grams brilliant ideas.

"Let's just walk around, keep our ears open and our faces hidden."

"Lead on," Lizzy said. "It can't get any worse."

We circled half of the arena, making our way through stinky pigeon coops, rabbit cages, and sweaty men in wife-beater shirts. We were gingerly treading through a maze of electrical cables when I looked up then blinked twice hoping I wasn't hallucinating. I wasn't.

I elbowed Lizzy. "Harry Whodunit."

"Where?" She whiplashed her head.

"Coming this way. Talking to some guy. We need to let them get by us then follow him to see what he's up to."

Three of the cables ran through a mesh curtain-covered doorway. I grabbed Lizzy's arm. "Quick! Let's duck in here."

We stepped into a room filled with props for an act. A mounted circus-sized poster of an old airplane stood on my right. Just below the faded plane, figures of men fell from the open plane door into the clouds. Before I could take further inventory I heard Harry's whiney voice approaching.

Lizzy and I stood side-by-side. The mesh curtain allowed us to see the little creep

but the shadows prevented him from seeing us—not that he was looking. He strolled by with a young guy dressed in khakis and a white polo shirt. Two friends just shooting the breeze.

A few of Harry's words reached me as they passed. "My father's ticked. He knows I placed that ad for you. Next time do your own investigating!"

I couldn't believe it. Gram's half-baked idea was actually paying off. A real lead. We needed to follow them and find out who Harry's friend was.

A strong hand clamped on my shoulder.

CHAPTER 27

 turned my head toward Lizzy. A gnarly hand was clamped on her shoulder also.

"Just in time!" The voice belonged to a thirtyish guy with a lacquered pompadour and wearing a shabby black Elvis jumpsuit. It was a *pinch me moment.*

"The plane is waiting for you two at the north end of the parking lot," he said. "We'll take off and head out over the shoreline. Hope you know what you're doing. Don't have time to train new recruits."

The grabber was at least six-feet tall, with plastic-like hair, narrow eyes, bushy black brows and jaggedy teeth. He extended his hand. "Alvin." His grip was firm, his hand rough. This was a man who performed manual labor not magic.

"Olive and Lizzy." I pointed to Lizzy.

He removed his hands and reached in his pocket. "Here's your earplugs. I'll strap you into the harnesses when we get on the plane. Don't be put off by old Jenny's looks—she's a Skyvan. If you haven't wing-walked one she has a roar when she takes off and her assent is slow-ish but don't let that throw you. She ain't fallin' from the sky."

My left eye started twitching. I pressed my finger to my lid.

"Jenny's built to hold twenty-two jumpers but right now we're down to ten. If you look over your shoulders while you're wing-walking, you'll see the skydivers drop from the rear exit cargo door just like in the movies. It's a beautiful sight."

Alvin placed his hands on our backs and pushed us in a direction I was certain we didn't want to go. "Jenny can take off and land almost anywhere. The beach can be rough but she can handle it."

I felt Lizzy tug my belt.

"This is a dry run—just you two wing walkers. You'll go up with the troop tomorrow for final rehearsal."

"Did he say wing walkers?" Lizzy whispered.

Speechless—I nodded.

A little diversionary chatter was needed while I collected my thoughts. "Are those flying Elvis's on the poster?"

He shook his head. "Flying Alvins. That's the whole troop— well not really—we lost Joe, Jim, and Zeke."

Lizzy clutched my hand.

"Show time we fly over the arena. You gals stay on the wings. The guys jump out in a free-fall and then open their underarm chutes. The kids love it."

"Skydiving is a stunt. How does it qualify as magic?" Harry was getting away but I was leery of cutting Alvin short. There was something in his eyes and it wasn't sawdust.

"Nothing magic about skydiving. The Magicians' Fusion needed a grand finale. I was in the right place at the right time." He grinned exposing his creepy teeth.

I backed away placing my hand protectively in front of Lizzy. The hairs on the back of my neck prickled.

Alvin brushed one hand against the other. "I used to work back stage at the arena doing the heavy lifting. Weekends I spent skydiving for fun. The magicians put out a call for a final act. Something different. I brought my diving friends in billed as the *Flying Alvins*. They hired us on the spot. We've worked the show for sixteen years."

"Did you ever hear of a guy called the Masked Dangler?" I watched his eyes, the spinning motion of his pupils mesmerizing. Might as well pick what was left of his brain.

"You're friends of the Masked Dangler!" Alvin's eyeballs came to rest in twin dots of admiration. He took a moment to process. "That Masked Dangler feller ain't been around for a bit. I've been fiddling with side jobs and lost track of time."

Alvin scratched the tip of his nose. "You know how it is—a rabbit here, a half-a-lady there. But magic ain't like the high of the *Flying Alvins*. If you got a connection with the Dangler, he'd be a showstopper."

He closed his eyes lost in a vision. "I can see it now. *The Flying Alvins,* you gals, and the Dangler!"

While his eyes were closed I peeked out the curtain. Harry Whodunit was nowhere in sight. A door stood open—I could see the parking lot. A quick jaunt away.

I motioned to Lizzy and while Alvin remained in dream land we made our getaway.

Wing walkers indeed.

"Zig-zag so he can't see us!" Lizzy and I picked up speed with each step.

"Get behind that carnival wagon!" I shoved her out of sight, stumbling after her. We weren't being followed. "My car's to the right. Ready?"

Lizzy grabbed my wrist. "What do you think of that Whodunit tidbit we overheard?"

"Rex Marchmain didn't have anything to do with the challenge. We have to find the guy who was with Whodunit. Since we don't know who he is, we have to find Whodunit and drag it out of him."

My phone jangled at my hip reminding me that I hadn't checked my voicemail after my phone rang when I was in the tube.

We dashed to my car. Hot as a pizza oven. We opened the doors to let out the heat. While we waited for the temperature to drop below molten, I checked my voicemail. One from Grams.

I put my phone on speaker. "Olive? I can't reach Lizzy. Pam and I are sitting in a limo in the parking lot at your shop with some foreign guy. It's just after seven. Got lots to tell you. Hurry!"

As I pocketed my phone I caught sight of Harry Whodunit's buddy. I scanned the lot—Khaki Pants was alone. "We're not going to get a chance like this again! We have to grab that guy!"

Lizzy didn't hesitate. One of the many things I loved about her was that she would follow me over the cliff, up the mountain, or across a parking lot to tackle a total stranger.

We closed in on Khaki Pants.

CHAPTER 28

"*E*xcuse me, sir!" I semi-yelled.

Khaki Pants turned in my direction and paused, giving me a chance to memorize his looks in case he decided to bolt. Late twenties—slender build, sand-colored hair, a light tan, and green eyes.

Had to give the guy credit—he didn't take off running at the sight of two female Elvis-styled floozies charging him. Considering the vapid vaudeville going on inside, we were probably the norm.

With an air of authority I held up my hand. "We're associated with the Starfish Cove Police Department." Lizzy jabbed me with her elbow.

"Covert operation. I understand you caused an ad to be placed in the *Silverfish Gazette* challenging the Masked Dangler to a dangle-off." I wiped the sweat from my forehead and loosened my Elvis collar. "I'm Olive. This is Lizzy."

"You're with the police?" He gave us the once over with cynical eyeballs.

"COPP" I said, resting my hand on the small purse clipped to my low-slung belt. In some alternate reality it might be mistaken for a holster.

"I'm a journalist," he said. "I'm used to dealing with the police—never heard of COPP. What's that stand for?"

"Citizens On Patrol Plus. Besides traffic control we handle blackmail and the occasional homicide." It was worth a try.

He laughed out loud.

"What's your name and your connection to the Masked Dangler?" I said. "You can tell us here or at the police station. While you're at it—how do you know Harry—Marchmain—Whodunit?"

He reached in his pocket. If he was going for a gun we were in trouble. Lizzy and I didn't have a can of hairspray between us.

Khaki Pants pulled out a business card and handed it to me. It read Sam Silas — Investigative Reporter—*Miami Herald*.

His name jumped out at me. "Any relation to *The Great Silas?*"

"My grandfather. I'm gathering material for a book on his life and times. I met Harry Whodunit in the course of poking around Starfish Cove."

"Why'd you have Whodunit place that challenge ad?" Lizzy asked. "We overheard you talking to the twerp."

He smirked. "You ladies look trustworthy and you are COP... Ps. If I'd placed that ad it might lead back to me—arouse suspicion. Whodunit had already inserted himself in the magic community and he's dying to assume the Dangler title."

"Why did you care about the Masked Dangler?" This Sam guy was no fool. He'd probably worked out most of the puzzle. He just needed confirmation.

"During the course of my investigation I deduced the Masked Dangler had something to do with the way my grandfather died. If the challenge enticed the codger out of retirement I'd get my hands on him. Shake the truth out of him."

His story was plausible.

"Trust me. I'm not into hocus-pocus. I just deal in facts. *The Great Silas'* love of magic didn't pass on. My father was a hedge fund manager—made money disappear—but that was as close to magic as we came."

"Do you think *The Great Silas* was murdered?"

Sam nodded. "I spent five months working with Scotland Yard's cold case division. The props that killed my grandfather were kept in the London Museum of Magic. The Yard's forensic people are certain they were tampered with—causing his death. The most obvious clue was the linchpin that prevented the blade from moving had been sawed halfway through." He rubbed his barely-there stubble. "Interesting, huh?"

"We suspected he was murdered." I should have bit my tongue.

Lizzy gave me another elbow shot. I was in danger of giving up Nelson Dingler.

"You know about *The Great Silas's* murder?"

"We handle the occasional cold case," Lizzy said. It was my turn to give her an elbow poke. We'd pressed the fib button one too many times.

"I'm late for an appointment," Sam said. "You have my card—call me. Let's get together for lunch. You gals might have something I can use in my book. I'll make it worth your time."

I turned to see Lizzy dash back to my car. Was she worried about Grams and Pam or was she afraid for her father's reputation? I ran after her, slipped behind the wheel, started the car, turned the air conditioning to high and closed my door. "Any thoughts on Sam Silas?"

Lizzy slammed her door. "If he builds a case against my father and writes his book, the Dingler name will be mud."

"You're a Kelly now—by marriage—but I understand how you feel. Neither you nor Grams or Pam can be blamed for what your father may have done—probably did do. One rotten egg in a dozen doesn't make the other eleven stink."

"Not unless the shell is cracked wide open." Lizzy leaned over and turned the air vents onto her face.

"Any idea who that foreign guy could be holding your grandmother hostage in a limo in the parking lot of *Nonna's Cold Cream?*" The question came out in one long breathless rush.

"More likely Grams is holding him hostage, but no—I can't even guess. Maybe she met him at the Yacht Club. Step on it!"

Five miles over the speed limit was the best I dared do—getting pulled over was not an option. Dressed in our Elvis jumpsuits and painted like hussies, Kal was bound to hear about a traffic stop within minutes. Even double-speak wouldn't cover the explanation.

Dusky dark spread a lingering purple haze over the Gulf, it felt like an omen as I drove down Starfish Boulevard. My heart lodged in my throat. My right leg shook—unsteady on the pedals.

If I had to explain myself to me I couldn't. It felt like the crescendo to the music in a horror movie. Something big was about to come down or maybe I was just hungry.

The nightlights illuminated the shop. A dark stretch limousine with tinted windows parked sideways at the front steps.

Friends of Myron?

CHAPTER 29

I blocked the limo with my car. If this was a kidnapping, it wasn't going to go down easy. Holding a ninety-four year old lady locked up in a luxury sedan—how low can you get?

Lizzy leapt from the car. I ran around and joined her. We were about to yank the passenger doors when one popped open and a male figure emerged silhouetted by the interior car lights.

A quick glimpse of Grams sitting with a champagne glass in her hand. I cut my eyes to the backlit guy who'd exited the car.

"Fabio!" The sight of Sophia Napoli's bodyguard sent a flush of relief flooding through me. The visions of Myron's minions and deadly danglers evaporated in a poof.

Sophia told us Fabio would visit our shop and check out *Nonna's Cold Cream* as soon as she was settled in London. It had slipped my mind. Fabio was here to inspect our operation. Lizzy and I exchanged horrified looks. We'd blown the endorsement deal.

The expression on Fabio's face was a collage of question marks. Our tiny shop would be understandable as a fledgling business but our jumpsuits, painted faces, and flibbertygibbet hair could never be associated with an international film star.

My makeup began to thicken, itching as if a thousand ants crawled over my cheeks. Humidity or humiliation?

"Miss Olive. Miss Lizzy." Fabio took each of our hands in turn. "Please step inside my car." He moved aside beckoning us to enter the limo.

Grams took the last gulp from her champagne flute and muffled a ladylike belch with her hand. "Lots to tell you," she said. She reached for the bottle sitting in the ice bucket.

Pam put her hand over the bottle and slid the bucket out of Grams' reach.

She did enjoy a glass of champagne now and then. "Just one more," she grumbled.

Pam shook her head. "Not tonight."

Fabio followed us into the limo, pulling the door closed—the lights softened to a candlelight glow. He settled into one of the seats. "It's more comfortable in here. Your grandmamma says there is no table inside your shop. Here we have more than one."

The table was on the table again. I could see a cold cream shop table in our future.

Twice the length of an ordinary sedan, with cushy black seats on both sides interrupted only by small shiny walnut counters— the car smelled of new leather and a hint of male cologne.

Fabio centered two flutes on the nearest end table and poured a glass for Lizzy and one for me. As he handed me the flute his eyes made lingering contact. Still processing the surprise I couldn't get a bead on him—was he curious or furious?

"It's impolite to remark on a lady's appearance and so I will say nothing about your tootsie costumes." I blushed. A man in a limo is like a man in a tuxedo—able to induce mini-quakes even in a quake-proof gal.

Our host handed Lizzy a glass. "Your grandmamma told me the

sad tale of her son's death. The criminal element was at one time familiar to me. I grew up in Naples and saw many bad things before Miss Sophia rescued me. She took me off the streets and into her employ. I promise what has happened to your family will be held separate and discreet from your beauty business."

I could have hugged Fabio. Sophia Napoli's endorsement might put *Nonna's Cold Cream* in lights—to lose it over Nelson's dangling would have been unfair.

"The tale of the dangling death is horrible. A man does not hang himself by his feet. I know of feet hangings but such things were done long ago to spread the fires of fear among the peasants."

He reached across the aisle and patted Lizzy's hand. "I will help you in whatever way I can."

"See! You don't have to worry about your business." Grams looked tired even as the excited words tumbled from her lips. We needed to get her home in her own little bed before she keeled over.

"Guess what Pam and I learned at the Yacht Club!" She motioned with her glass towards the bottle.

In a single swoop Pam took the champagne flute from Grams. "One glass will do."

"Who made you the boss of me?" Grams growled.

"I did." Pam said. "We've all had a long day. One glass is enough, Grams. Now tell Lizzy and Olive what we learned at the Yacht Club—or do you want me to do it?"

"It's my story. I'll tell it!" Grams crossed her arms over her chest. She looked like a half-plucked chicken facing off in the barnyard.

"Freddy the doorman at the club was on break. We took him across the street for coffee and Danish. They have the best blueberry—"

"Grams!" Pam cut her off.

"Turns out, according to Freddy, Rex Marchmain isn't happy

about being Commodore—not yet," Grams said. "He planned on taking his yacht across the Atlantic and sailing around the Mediterranean Sea for a year before the Commodore title came up for grabs."

Grams was on the same trail we'd just hiked but her intel on Rex Marchmain's plans confirmed his innocence. I poked my tongue into my cheek. Let her command the stage. Lizzy and I would fill in any gaps.

"The old fox married some young chippie around Christmas Time," Grams said. "He intended a delayed honeymoon—figured he had a couple of years before the Commodore post became vacant. Nelson's death threw a monkey wrench into his plans. He has to go after the title—now."

With a firm nod of her chin she pronounced her verdict. "As far as I can tell Rex Marchmain had nothing to do with Nelson's death. We hung around the Yacht Club for hours until we were getting suspicious looks, then we left."

"Guess who we met at the arena?" I said. *"The Great Silas'* grandson!"

"Ah hah!" Grams poked an index finger in the air. "The circle closes. Another magician!"

"Afraid not. He's a journalist—Sam Silas—researching his grandfather's history for a biography. Looking into old Silas' death. He convinced Harry Whodunit to place the ad thinking it would draw out the Masked Dangler."

Grams mouth fell open but nothing came out.

"He knows *The Great Silas's* equipment was tampered with," I said. "I think he suspects Nelson."

I cut my eyes to Lizzy. She squished her brows together but I went on anyway. "He wants to meet with us."

"Don't you dare!" Grams waggled her finger at us.

"May I interrupt, ladies?" Fabio said. "I want to do as Miss Sophia requested and inspect your operation. I have come at a bad time. Let us end this evening with my driver taking you to your homes. We shall pick you up in the morning. I would feel better if you did not drive after a single glass of champagne. Will your cars be safe here overnight?"

"Tsk!" Grams said. "This is Starfish Cove—the safest community in Florida!"

I choked on my last sip of champagne.

"So Miss Sophia's chauffeur and I will escort you to your doors. Shall we agree on a pickup time for tomorrow?"

Grams gave me a wiggly eyebrow. "Make it eleven. I'd like to sleep in."

She was fibbing through her dentures.

CHAPTER 30

$\mathcal{F}$abio helped Grams and Pam from the limo. The car took up most of her driveway. The curtains in the neighbor's house fluttered in a wave of curiosity. The sight of a limo in a neighborhood of cottages offered the equivalent of a panther lying amid a litter of kittens.

"I'll get her tucked in." Pam's whispered words were barely audible but nothing got past Grams.

"I heard that! I'm not a child, Pamela!" Grams slipped her arm in Fabio's and he walked her to the door.

Once Pam and Grams were safely inside Fabio returned to the car wearing a bemused smile. "Grandmothers come in three styles —prim and proper, motherly and smelling of the kitchen, or tough as Mafioso."

We laughed. He didn't have to pin a title on Grams—she owned it.

He settled back in the seats with a sigh. "And now, Miss Lizzy— directions please?"

"Have your driver get us back on Starfish Boulevard, up two miles, and turn into Shrimp Bay—he can only make a right unless you want to do some limo surfing in the moonlight."

Ten minutes later we were wending our way through the narrow streets, taking the corners in big sweeping turns. The limo made the final bend onto Kelp Circle.

"Your lights are on," I said, as we drew close.

"Heather's still at her friends." Lizzy said. "That's Dave's truck at the side of the house. I almost forgot what he looks like," she said, sighing heavily.

"Olive, how about you walk me to the door? No offense Fabio, but my friend Dave has a bad habit of jumping to conclusions. We look like we had a night on the town. A handsome Italian escort and his limo might push the limits of Dave's short temper."

Dave was too busy managing *Nancy's Fried Fish* to be jealous—nevertheless Lizzy's adventures often didn't sit well with him. After the hustle-bustle of the restaurant he sought a quiet domestic routine—a lifestyle alien to Lizzy. They were an odd match—a bear in a cave and a butterfly in the wind.

As our feet hit the front steps the door swung open. WonderDog lunged at Lizzy throwing his weight on her. With his front paws on her shoulders and his bushy tail wagging like the propeller on a helicopter, she lost her footing and fell against me.

WonderDog's wide-eyed look at the oversized car and the man standing beside it set him to barking. He ran at Fabio—who said something to him in Italian. The dog backed off, sat down, and continued to wag his tale. Evidently he was a multilingual hound.

Dave filled the doorway looking domestic in jeans, a T-shirt, and one of Lizzy's tea aprons. He wore an oven mitt on one hand and his usual pinched expression. He took a quick look at Lizzy and me in our Elvis outfits, bleary eyes, sticky makeup, and messy hair, and then his eyes cut past us to Fabio and the limo.

"Missed you, Sweetie, " Lizzy stood on tiptoe and gave him a peck on the cheek.

"How many questions do I get?" Dave said, not bothering to greet me. He always seemed to blame me for Lizzy's escapades.

"I'll explain it all after I've had a shower." She put her hand on his arm in a reassuring manner.

Dave limbered up his shoulders and neck—his eyes fixed on Fabio.

Lizzy gave him a wide-eyed look that caused me to dissolve in exhausted laughter.

"Before you go beating your chest with your fists, the guy by the limo is Sophia Napoli's bodyguard, and no we were not out partying." Lizzy said. "I'll introduce him, but please be nice. I'll explain everything later."

She motioned Fabio to approach.

"Fabio Santoro, this is Dave Bronson."

Extending his hand, Fabio allowed his eyes to slip to Dave's frilly apron.

"I insist all my men wear aprons." Lizzy attempted to break the tension of the moment.

An amused smile passed over Fabio's face. "I find wearing an apron adds to the joy of cooking."

The muscle in Dave's jaw popped—he'd yet to show any sign of a sense of humor in the time I'd known him. He shook hands with Fabio, threw in a curt "Nice to meet you." And disappeared into the house.

"Pick you up at about eleven as your grandmamma requested?" Fabio said. He tapped his lips with one finger. "Is there a reason to trouble your grandmother? She is not involved in your business, is that not so?"

"True. Our meeting is about *Nonna's Cold Cream*," I said trying to keep the relief from my voice. "We can meet earlier—say nine— show you the shop and demonstrate how we prepare the cream. It's important you know all the measures in place to insure the quality of our products."

"We can be done by eleven and take Grams and Pam to lunch," Lizzy said, sounding relieved. "Grams needs to slow down, she hasn't stopped since she found my father's…body."

"Nine it is. Have a good evening, Miss Lizzy."

"Don't bother about getting my clothes now," I said. "I'll have this jumpsuit cleaned and collect my things tomorrow."

Lizzy gave me a feeble smile. "Just throw the jumpsuit away. That's what I'm going to do with the one I wore. I'll never wear those things again."

"It's going to work out. I promise." I waved goodbye.

Fake optimism didn't come easy. The purple shadow lingered over my shoulder. Someone had murdered Nelson Dingler and I was no closer to finding the killer—although I'd eliminated Rex Marchmain and probably his idiot son from my list of suspects.

Fabio and I settled back in the limo, gave the driver directions to my place and cruised up the boulevard.

"More champagne?"

"Thank you, no. I feel I should apologize for this evening—from our sleazy outfits to Dave's rude behavior."

"You have nothing to apologize for. First, you did not expect me. Second, I had a cousin in Naples who worked with the police. She often dressed much more provocatively to catch thieves and murderers. And as far as Miss Lizzy's Dave—if another man caught me in my apron, I would have reacted quite similarly."

"I can't imagine you being impolite."

"Can you imagine me as a good listener? Perhaps I can help you sort out your clues."

"Thank you—not tonight. I'm exhausted."

As the limo pulled up to the front of my building, I glimpsed Kal sitting in his unmarked car in the parking lot. He had to know I saw him—the security lights from the building cast a spotlight on him.

"Don't walk me to my door," I said to Fabio. "I'll pop in the elevator and wave from the balcony so you know I made it. I insist." I extended my hand as he leaned in—no doubt intending to plant a continental kiss on my cheek.

"See you tomorrow." I said softly. By shaking his hand I was able to keep him at a distance.

It wasn't the humidity wilting me as I rode up to my floor. My last text to Kal pinged like a tiny neon sign every word glowing with guilt. "Can't meet tonight—something personal came up. Unavoidable. Will connect in the morning. Not to worry."

Something personal. Unavoidable. Ugh. There was no reason why I should feel guilty. Kal was doing his job while I was doing mine. He found a match for the soap on the rope while I had been working undercover. Fabio was here on business. How could anyone misinterpret what I did?

I scurried to my door, turned, and leaned on the walkway railing looking down at the parking lot. Two sets of guy eyes were on me. I waved down at Fabio but pretended not to notice Kal still sitting in his car. Once in my condo, I closed the door behind me and held my breath hoping Kal wouldn't knock, call, or text.

He didn't.

CHAPTER 31

*S*leep refused to come. Something nibbled at my mind. It had been there since—if I remembered when, I'd remember what.

Puff nuzzled her cold button nose under my earlobe. Her purring coupled with the gentle sound of the waves would normally lull me to sleep. Perhaps it was the boost from the champagne that kept me awake—but I'd only had one glass.

The open window allowed the sweet, slightly fishy breeze to waft over my face. Strangely, the image of a key played in my mind —it refused to leave. I rolled on my side staring into Puff's big blue eyes. "Know anything about keys?" She licked my cheek.

I studied symbolism my first year at college. What had I learned in my iconography class about keys? A key represents opening doors of opportunities. It represents knowledge, mystery, and initiation. Sometimes a key can mean the difference between life and death—between freedom and prison. If it's given as a gift it's meant to open doors, if it's taken from someone it's meant to invade their secrets.

A bolt of adrenalin shot through me. A key is the key to the killer. Irma wore one around her neck.

The clock read just after nine. I popped out of bed called Lizzy as I paced with excitement. "New plan. I'm on to something. I'll pick you up at eight in the morning. Have Grams and Pam meet us at your father's apartment."

"What's up?"

"Tell you when I see you—just in case this is all a crazy dream and I'm not really talking to you right now. At this point I can't tell if I'm awake or asleep. Just on idea overload."

"How much champagne did you have?"

"Less than one glass."

"What about Fabio? Isn't he set to pick us up?"

"Crumbcakes! All our cars are at the shop! I'll figure something out."

Fabio caught the phone after the first ring. "Something has come up. I hate to ask but can we meet later in the day?"

"Is this about Miss Lizzy's father? Do you need my help?"

"No. Yes! I could use your help. Could your chauffeur pick me up at seven-thirty tomorrow morning? I've got to get my car."

"Certainly. He'll be there. Is there any other way I might help? I am a bodyguard."

It was so cute the way he said it I almost laughed. "The fewer people involved the better."

Fewer people brought Kal to mind. I put him on my maybe list. If I was going to expose the killer it would take a gentle touch. Kal could be a bull plus he had a broom up his back about legal-schmegal ways to do things. I'd only call him if we got in a jam.

Impossible to sleep, I paced the apartment, stood on the balcony and watched the moonlit waves wash in and out. I warmed some milk in a tiny pot remembering it was something Nonna did when sleep eluded her. I sat at the kitchen table, and sipped from a mug.

Relaxing thoughts wiggled away like a herd of caterpillars. Sheep refused to be counted and memories of pleasant vacations evaporated, if only tomorrow would come.

Puff scrambled in my lap mewing. "Cows' milk is not good for kitties." I finally caved to her persistence and dabbed a drop on her nose. She licked it off sharing a look of delight. "That's it for now, kid!"

I needed sleep if I was going to be at the top of my game.

My phone pinged a text message from Kal. It was guaranteed to irritate me. No sense in reading it. I'd never get to sleep. Ready to shut the phone off, curiosity got the better of me.

His message was so terse he could have sent it in Morse code. Conveying emotions in a text message is like capturing lightning bolts in a bottle. It can't be done.

Personal? Unavoidable?
Step back from this case.

If Kal would stop lurking about, his feelings might not get hurt.

I scooped up Puff and crawled back into bed snuggling her. Sometime during the night I must have dozed. When I opened my eyes the soft morning light was peeking in the window. The clock read seven-oh-five. It couldn't be!

With the speed of an animated cartoon, I managed to feed and water Puff, jump in and out of the shower, and run a brush through my hair in less than twenty minutes. A dab of magic cold cream under each eye and the remaining raccoon shadows disappeared. Good to go or as good as it was going to get.

Unsure what the day held, I opted for my usual standby...black slacks and black cotton T-shirt. I was just about to dash out the door when my phone rang. Fabio's chauffeur was downstairs waiting.

I pressed the elevator button, hummed a short tune, and waited as the doors opened to reveal Ivy LaVine, former friend now ticked off neighbor.

"Good morning!" I said in a cheerful tone.

She gave me a blank look. It wasn't until the doors opened on the first floor that she said, "Have a good day."

As I settled into the limo I realized Ivy stood in the lobby door with her eyes fixed on me. The possible scenarios that were running through her mind made me chuckle. I sat back and enjoyed the brief ride to the shop catching glimpses of the Gulf waters between the high-rise condos.

My Prius sat alongside the Dingler ladies' cars. The beach sand blown across Starfish Boulevard left a light coat of grit, but otherwise it was just as I had left it.

I headed over to Lizzy's house.

CHAPTER 32

*L*izzy was ready to go when I pulled into her driveway. She ran down her front stairs with WonderDog at her heels. "I can't bear to leave him home again. He's reading my stress, poor pup wants to help."

"Why not? WonderDog's our hero."

I grinned at Lizzy's outfit. "You read my mind." She was wearing black Capri pants and a short sleeve black T-shirt. It would go well with our logoed *Nonna Cold Cream* jackets. "When we meet Fabio at the shop we'll wear our smocks—keep it very professional."

WonderDog jumped into the back of the Prius. Lizzy slid in the front and we were off.

"Grams and Pam are set to meet us. A neighbor took them to get their cars from the shop. Are you going to tell me now or make me wait?"

"I may be way off base but I don't think so. Bear with me—I'm thinking out loud."

WonderDog leaned over the seat—all ears.

"When Irma stopped in the shop yesterday, she told me she and

Cosmos were leaving today but might try one more time to send your father's celestial being to that planet she's promoting."

"She'd need to get in the apartment and for that she'd need Grams."

I cut Lizzy a quick glance. "Unless she has her own key. Did your father change the locks when she moved out? I'm certain I locked the door before she came in after us and started fumbling around the apartment—supposedly sending Nelson's spirit to some planet she calls Karma."

"So Irma still has a key to the apartment."

"She has more than the front door key. Did you notice the key she wears around her neck?"

I could almost hear Lizzy thinking. "Not until you just mentioned it. She does wear quirky little charms on a chain. The key is antique—right?"

"Hang on—concentrating on parking."

I hesitated before pulling into the two vacant spots in front of Nelson's building. If Irma planned a visit she might recognize my car. I didn't want to scare her off. "Call Grams while I circle the block. Tell her to park out of sight."

Whoever invented one-way streets had some serious anti-social problems. Because of them I drove around the corner, hit the one-way street, and circled around it a second time. I finally found a space in the Pocket Change Bank's employees' lot—hoping I wouldn't get towed.

"Grams, just listen. It's important you not park in front of Father's building." Lizzy covered the phone and rolled her eyes. "I understand you've already parked. We're in the bank's parking lot —employee side. Un-park and come here. Olive will explain."

Lizzy made a yammering mouth with her hand. "They won't tow you. If they do, I'll pay for it." Pause. "Yes—and any damages to your car. I promise." Another pause. "Yes I know it's not easy to find parts for your classic car."

Grams' faded gold Edsel took the entry curb angling up and then dropping down with a thud. Moby Dick looking for Captain Ahab. As the car headed toward us all I could see was the top of the hula-hoop steering wheel and two tiny fists plus the look of terror on Pam's face.

I pointed to the space next to mine and Grams whipped the ginormous car snuggly into place. It was sure to get towed as it stuck out from all the conservative compacts like a whale in a fish tank.

As Grams and Pam debarked, I half-whispered to Lizzy. "If Irma shows up I'm going to need you and Pam to keep Grams off her. If I can get Irma alone I'll get into her head."

"You think she killed my father?"

"What are you two whispering about?" Grams asked. "Why all the cloak, dagger, and bank parking?"

"We may have a visitor. I didn't want to discourage her with the sight of our cars."

Grams smacked her palms together. "Her? It's Irma! I knew it."

"Irma told me she and that Cosmos fellow were going to make one more try at sending Nelson's celestial being to the planet Karma," I said.

All of Grams' nonagenarian energy was back. She was ready to rock 'n roll. In her tan leggings, brown feather-printed dress, and brown orthopedic shoes she looked like a little wren but I'd learned not to underestimate the lady. More hawk than wren, she turned on her heels, fists at her sides and marched between the parked cars.

"Wait up!" I took off after her. WonderDog and Pam scrambled to catch up with us.

We converged at the elevator. I said, "If Irma shows up I need some private time with her. We have no real evidence. If she feels we're ganging up on her she'll clam up."

"You're the shrink," Grams said, patting me on the back.

We rode up to the sixth floor. The yellow tape was now double-taped to the door. Kal was going to go ballistic no matter how this turned out.

Grams fought her way through the yellow tape lacking only a machete to clear a perfect path. I locked the door behind us.

Someone had been in, dusted, and picked up the broken pieces of the crystal vase.

If we were going to spy on Irma we needed to hide. The furthest room from the foyer was the master bedroom. I herded Grams' gang in and pulled the door halfway closed.

CHAPTER 33

*G*rams flipflopped about Irma. "Looks like a bedroom, feels like a prison. I'm not too sure I should have agreed to this. Let's wait for her out there and grab her when she comes in."

"Please," I said, "let's get back on track. Did you notice the key around Irma's neck?"

She rubbed the bridge of her nose. "Can't say that I did. What's it look like?"

"Small. Old. Antique. She wears a couple of charms on the same chain. She described it as the key to her journey to the planet Karma. Any idea what that key might open? Did Nelson have any hidden panels in the apartment?"

"Not that I know of but my son was a need-to-know person. He could have an elephant hidden behind the walls. It would be pretty smelly by now."

"It would have to be more valuable than an elephant to entice Irma," Lizzy said.

Pam pushed up the sleeves of her *Nurses Rule!* sweatshirt. "Should we start hunting?"

I shook my head. "We have to be careful not to scare her off. If she comes to the door and hears us she'll run. I'm guessing she'll try for an early start and then head back to wherever. Let's be patient."

The clock on the nightstand read eight-twenty. We settled in, Grams lying on Nelson's bed with Pam sitting at the foot. Lizzy took an armchair while WonderDog sat at her feet. I paced.

The deactivated intrusion alarm binged and then binged again indicating the front door opened and closed. I put my finger to my lips as the Dingler ladies and WonderDog perked up.

I tiptoed to the bed and whispered, "Let her snoop. Maybe she'll find whatever that key fits." I looked around the bedroom— there was no place for us to hide if Irma opened the door. With a double hand flip I shooed the gang into the master bathroom.

WonderDog gave me a quizzical look. What new game were we playing? Ever so silently we stuffed our party of four plus a hound into the huge master bathroom. Huddled together trying not to breathe, I felt like a kid playing hide-and-seek.

The sounds coming through indicated Irma had help—probably Cosmos.

The searching continued with banging on the walls and drawers slamming shut. The sounds got louder as they started on the master bedroom.

Steam came out of Grams' ears. Her late son's home was being violated and she was having none of it. She uttered a low growl.

WonderDog glanced up at her and then at me—his expression conveying *if she can why can't I?*

Before I could rein her in, Grams reached the bathroom door at the exact moment Cosmos pushed it open. It was with a combination of her momentum and anger that she reached up and yanked at the cultist's long blond hair.

Cosmos yelped from surprise and pain as WonderDog, protecting Grams, bit him somewhere in the middle of his caftan.

He kicked out sending WonderDog reeling backwards as his blond hair came off in Grams' hand revealing a shaved noggin.

Ivy had described the soap buyer as a young guy with a shaved head. The soap on the rope was yet another question to be answered during my upcoming confrontational analysis session.

Irma didn't know it yet but I was about to dig into her delusions, glue together her disjointed justifications, and find out if she killed Nelson.

I'd come to like Irma despite my instincts. I needed to understand how she got around me—I was supposed to be good at reading people. Where did my mojo go? I don't like being conned and she'd either tricked me or hypnotized me. I wasn't turning her over to Kal until I understood how I'd been fooled.

Outraged, Cosmos grabbed his wig from Grams. "Hair like this doesn't grow on trees!" He rubbed the spot where WonderDog had given him a souvenir.

"You're the dude who bought all our soap, aren't you?" I punched my finger into his chest.

"*The Irma* said to buy enough soap to coat a rope. How much soap does it take to coat a rope?" He shrugged. "Do you know? I don't. There's no shame in buying a couple of cases of soap. Not like I stole it. I paid cash. What's your problem lady?"

Irma stood behind his shoulder, looking surprisingly tranquil considering the situation. "We came back for my purse. I left it here."

"The front door was locked. Breaking and entering," Lizzy said as she, Pam, and Grams stepped toward Cosmos and Irma.

I pushed my way out of the bathroom and looped my arm under Irma's. This first round was all about winning her trust.

Cosmos bolted to the front door. "See you back at the commune!" He waved as he made his exit.

Pam and Lizzy were out the door after him in a flash.

"Let's sit in the living room." I said to Irma. "It's more comfortable there."

I escorted the cultist to the sofa and sat across from her. The muscles in my legs cramped as I held myself ready to nab her if she tried to escape.

Within minutes, the Dingler sisters returned without Cosmos. They looked flummoxed. "He's gone!" Pam said.

"He's not in the elevator or on the stairs," Lizzy appeared bewildered.

"Maybe he slipped into one of the doctors' offices downstairs?" I said. "He should be easy to find in a gynecologist's office."

"Maybe he's just a hologram." Irma said.

"We'll check out the offices. If he's there we'll grab him." Pam pushed up her errant sleeves.

Grams gave me a look laced with caution. "Take care, Olive." She picked up a brass candlestick from the sideboard, bouncing it in her hand as if to feel the weight of it.

"I'll stand outside this door," Grams said, still gripping the candlestick. "It doesn't take three of us to search for a guy wearing a caftan in a gynecologist office."

The Dinglers strode out of the apartment leaving me alone with *The Irma*.

CHAPTER 34

*P*rofessional pride demanded I get to the bottom of how Irma duped me. But I couldn't let that sidetrack me from learning about Nelson's death.

In truth, I didn't have enough evidence to connect her to the killing. Soap and an apartment key? Weaker than a third cup on a single teabag. This was going to take every rabbit I could pull out of my psychologist's hat.

"Your blue caftan conveys such peace. I can understand why you wear it. It makes you look like an angel. I see the little key on your necklace is different from the other charms. You said it unlocks your opportunity to journey to the planet Karma. That key almost brings something back to me from my childhood. It's calling to me. May I feel it?" I extended my hand expecting her to resist.

With a beatific smile, she said, "Of course." Irma unhooked the key from the chain and without hesitation handed it to me. Her cooperativeness made me uneasy. Was I the mouse and she the cat, allowing my silly requests until time to pounce?

I held the key in my hand avoiding a direct look into her eyes—

not that I believed she had the power to use some sort of hypnosis. "It feels very warm. How will it enable you to travel to the seven planets—to Karma?"

"That is not clear to me yet. I just know it will."

"Where did it come from?"

Irma smiled. "The oddest thing. As I readied Nelson's Remington painting for the buyer, my hand was pulled to the corner of the frame. I lifted the protective backing and found the key taped to the canvas. Power emanated from it but with a sense that I could convert that power to achieve the journey to the seven planets and Karma."

I wasn't about to debate the pros and cons of being beamed up to a planet that may not even have the basic necessities like dental floss and dark chocolate. "Do you think Nelson knew about the key?"

"I'm certain the monster put it there. It wasn't the painting he valued but this key. It's the key to a fortune and power here on earth and to me the power to complete my mission of getting my people to Karma."

"What fortune?" I tried not to look in her eyes—but felt my guard slipping.

"That's what I'm here to find out. I'm entitled to whatever it is." Irma leaned forward. "The fortune will support us here until the power sends us on our ultimate journey."

Not asking for the return of the key told me she felt she held the upper hand, that she could take it whenever she wanted. Had she forgotten about Grams with the candlestick?

"Tell me about your marriage to Nelson."

"First, what do you see in my eyes?" She said in a whispery voice.

I took a chance. My willpower had to be stronger than hers— for one thing I could never be tempted to wear a sky-blue caftan.

Her eyes turned the color of clouds—soft and harmless. I said, "I see you're about to tell me the truth."

"You can be trusted, Olive. I knew it from our first meeting." She closed her eyes and shuddered as if drawing on memories. When she opened them, her cloud-like eyes had turned to dark storms.

"Nelson was a monster. The two years we were married were hell on earth. I was a virtual prisoner of his moods. Sometimes I feared for my life."

"How long after you were married did he turn ugly?"

"The day after the ceremony he went into one of his dark states —it was as if he needed to unburden himself. He told me about his career in magic and how he was hated at the Magician's Hat because all those second-rate magicians were jealous of his abilities. In the midst of his tirade he revealed he was the Masked Dangler."

That floored me. He must have been having a breakdown. "He told you that deep dark secret?"

"He bragged about how he got revenge on his enemies by blackmailing them. Then he threatened me with his supposed mystic powers. It was as if once he confessed his sins, he needed to destroy me."

She locked eyes with me. "Does that make sense?"

Normally patients become emotional when revealing something so distressful, but aside from the one shudder, Irma remained calm.

"It's not uncommon for a confessor to resent the confessee," I said.

The storms in her eyes morphed into an indistinct redness. "He told me how he collected magicians' secrets in a journal."

I refrained from reaching out a comforting hand. That would have placed the key within her reach and the change in her eyes worried me. "You should have told someone and extricated your-self from that perilous situation."

"Eventually I did. It took one final menace to launch me into action. Nelson threatened to hang me by my feet from the chandelier and that he'd golf while I hung upside down. I'll never forget the vicious expression on his face when he said he'd play thirty-six holes."

In spite of my growing unease, my heart went out to her.

"I played the obedient wife waiting for my chance. That chance came with the arrival of the Cosmic Travelers."

"How did you come to be connected with them?"

"How does it go? When the student is ready, the teacher will arrive? The Cosmic Travelers found me. They taught me all they knew, and then I founded the Seven Planets. I became the woman you see before you."

I kept any sign of judgment from my expression. "You mentioned something about the cot?"

"That was where I was forced to sleep whenever I didn't do Nelson's bidding—whenever I was a naughty little wife. Only fitting that when I took all his possessions I left him only the cot."

"So the cot was symbolic," I said. "And when you dangled him from the chandelier, that was symbolic also?"

The redness in her eyes intensified. "Trippy poetic justice! Cosmos and I caught the monster by surprise. Stupefied, he let us in when we rang. Maybe he thought I was returning to his warm embrace."

The key cut into my palm as I tightened my fist around it.

"I showed Nelson the key and asked him what it was for," Irma said. "He refused to tell me and threatened instead to dangle me if I didn't give it back. He grabbed for the chain. Big mistake."

My breath became ragged as the redness continued to darken.

"Cosmos is skilled in the martial arts. He can knock a person out in seconds by pressing on their carotid artery."

She glanced over at the chandelier. "I guess you know that gaudy thing raises and lowers by a motor for maintenance access. Nelson was unconscious when Cosmos and I hung him by his feet."

Kal had mentioned something about a button in the service closet—one to adjust the height of the chandelier.

Irma continued, "When Nelson came around—upside down—he was forced to inhale the sweet smell of Lizzy's success. Your lavender soap. I taunted him with it. Knowing his daughter's slippery creation stopped him from climbing upright on the rope—he went berserk. He held Lizzy back her entire life. Unbeknownst to her, she'd turned the tables on him."

I couldn't help but ask, "Why'd you need so much soap?"

"Cosmos is not the brightest star in the sky. He bought all the soap you had—just in case."

"So Nelson was helpless *and* apoplectic?"

"The fool still refused to tell us what the key was for—just said it was his fortune. Chump that he was he said if he got his hands on me he was going to dangle me till I choked."

She ran her hand around over her neck. "We never intended for Nelson to die. We just left him to dangle until he gave up and told us what we wanted to know."

This time I detected a twinge of regret on her face as she studied the chandelier.

She sighed. "The Seven Planets rule in ironic ways. Cosmos and I split up to search the apartment for anything the key might fit. When we came back to prod Nelson—try again to get him to talk—he was dead."

Irma didn't intend to kill Nelson, but she did. And she had to pay. I had to delay her until Lizzy and Pam returned so we could hold her for Kal.

"Why did you marry him in the first place? You must have seen signs of his brute temperament?" How long before Lizzy and Pam returned?

"We're all put on this earth to learn at least one lesson. Nelson was mine. I made excuses for his behavior before we married—certain my love could change him."

She shrugged. "Strong as love is it can't change a person. I don't know where I'd be if I hadn't found my calling with the Seven Planets. Now I must ask you to return the key."

I was trying to come up with another delaying question when the redness in her eyes changed to boiling cauldrons. Snapping from calm kitten to snarling tiger, she

lunged at me.

CHAPTER 35

*I*rma threw herself on me, knocking me to the floor. I brought my foot up to push her away. My shoe got tangled in the yards of blue caftan and brought her down on top of me. I was trapped under a cult queen.

If I screamed for Grams, she'd run in and bring the brass candlestick down on Irma's head—killing her.

Worse yet, I couldn't risk calling a nonagenarian to my defense. If something happened to Grams I'd never forgive myself. I kept my mouth shut despite

Irma having at least forty-pounds on me and being in a lunatic frenzy that made her even stronger.

Our almost silent tussle continued for what seemed like hours as she tried to wrest the key from my hand. Over the sound of my blood pounding in my ears, I heard scratching and crunching.

Aiming for Irma's eye with my finger, I missed and stabbed her in the cheek.

She yelped and backed off.

"Sorry! I was trying to poke you in the eye."

As she renewed her efforts to out-wrestle me for the key, a

slightly-smelly, furry beast rammed her. WonderDog! He must have been trapped in the bathroom and managed to shred his way to freedom.

His momentum knocked her off me. I scrambled to my feet. She rolled away from the hero hound.

Recalling how readily he obeyed her command at the shop I couldn't count on him to keep her at bay. The fingers of my right hand ached from clutching the key. My nails dug crescent-shaped welts into my palm.

Irma pushed herself onto her knees.

"No you don't, Missy!" Grams burst through the door looking like a mini Statue of Liberty with the candlestick held high over her head.

"Grams, no. Don't! You'll kill her!"

"What's your point?" she barked.

Irma stood and moved toward me, obviously not ready to give up on the key.

WonderDog chomped down on the hem of Irma's caftan jerking his head back and forth like a rat-catcher.

Irma looked down at him and said, "Sit!"

He did.

Lizzy and Pam rushed in the door and ran to my side.

"Grab Irma!" Grams shrieked at them.

Outnumbered, Irma looked about for a way to escape. She faked a run at the rose garden staircase, then dodged to the right, and ran out the open front door. She took to the stairs with all of us, including Grams with the candlestick, hot on her heels.

Irma galloped down the stairs at a good clip—considering the tripability of her long dress she made good time. She threw her weight against the lobby door, broke through, and picked up speed. The yards of sky-blue fabric made her look like a fast moving cloud come to earth. She ran down Central Avenue causing heads to turn and cars to screech to a halt.

"Wait! Irma!" I yelled as if I believed she would stop.

Pam and WonderDog led our posse—I followed with Lizzy wobbling on her wedgies. I could hear Grams hollering but dared not look back for fear of losing track of the killer cultist.

Where was she headed? When she visited our shop she arrived in a brown car—I glanced up the street. There were plenty of vehicles—some brown. Was she hoping for Cosmos to pick her up?

Irma bolted across the road, cutting through traffic and nearly smashing herself into a mini-van but safely making it to the other side.

WonderDog stopped at the curb and looked back at Lizzy.

Pam dodged through the traffic. A pickup truck screeched to a halt but not before Pam rolled off the fender with cat-like agility.

"You okay?" I yelled, running past her.

"Get her!" Pam screeched, rubbing her hip.

Lizzy was now running at my side. "Does she have the key?"

WonderDog came up beside Lizzy. I glanced down as she wiggle-wobbled along at high speed. "Watch the curb!"

She didn't and went flying, skidding along the sidewalk on her stomach with her arms outstretched and her palms upright. They stopped her from slamming her head into the brick wall where she finally came to rest.

I stopped to help her. Her arms were skinned and her chin was scraped. Her Capri pants protected her legs, but her ankle was already swelling. WonderDog licked her face.

"Did Irma kill my father?" she asked through a grimace of pain.

"Not intentionally, but she did."

"What's a little scratch? Let's get her!"

I pulled her to her feet. She leaned on me as I scanned the street. I saw the blue caftan flow down the stairs that led to the Magician's Hat.

CHAPTER 36

"Why is she going in there?" Lizzy said, as she limped along leaning heavily on me.

"She knows the magicians are Nelson's enemies. She may have already talked to them. She's going to them for help."

WonderDog charged ahead leaving us in his wake. His Brillo-like body disappeared down the stairs. Nothing could stop that dog—except Irma's commands.

"You're hurt!" Pam caught up with us, holding her hip with one hand.

I left Lizzy and Pam to hobble along and sprinted to the Hat.

The moldy steps were slipperier than I remembered. I grabbed the grimy metal railing with my left hand, still gripping Irma's key in my right. Carefully planting one foot after the other I entered the cigar-smoke contaminated and mildewed magicians' haven.

The ever-slimy Bart Bottom, still in his tuxedo-printed T-shirt stood in front of me.

"You still looking for Harry? You're out of luck. No one here except me." His lie as obvious as his comb-over.

A snarl from WonderDog came from behind the stage curtain

—the same one we'd crawled under while chasing Whodunit. I pushed past Bottom.

Déjà vu all over again. The full body slide worked before so I tried it again—a splintery glide along the wooden floor and under the musty velveteen.

I rolled to my feet. Same dusty magician props as before. No Irma in sight.

WonderDog lay growling in front of the blue, red, and yellow phone booth-looking thing adorned with the evil man-in-the-moon face and the word *Vanish*.

I smiled. *Vanish* wasn't an appropriate word for Irma. She trapped herself by hiding in there.

Lizzy, Pam, and—amazingly enough—candlestick-wielding Grams clambered under the curtain.

As they stood—Grams using the candlestick as an aid—I put my forefinger to my lips and pointed at the Vanish Booth.

I stepped toward the booth and saw WonderDog's jaws clamp on a piece of sky-blue material sticking out from under the door.

Perfect. She wasn't going anywhere once we opened it. I said, "Irma, come out peacefully. We're all here and WonderDog's anchoring your caftan."

Irma's voice came out of the Vanish Booth. "WonderDog, sit!"

Darned if he didn't heed her again, dropping the caftan hem and going to a sitting position. The material swooshed under the door. No matter, she wasn't going to get by the three of us when we opened the door. Not to mention Grams itching to bop her with the candlestick.

I yanked the door open. Empty! I yelled, "Check the backdoor!" Whodunit had gotten

out that way. I pounded the walls hoping to trigger the secret exit that had to be there.

Lizzy stuck her head in the booth. "She didn't get out that way. The backdoor's padlocked."

"Impossible!" I said. "Pam, check the padlock and make sure it's not a trick lock. "

"Never mind, Pam." Lizzy said. "I already did that. It's a real lock and a real door."

"Then there must be a trapdoor under my feet. She got out of here somehow. She was in here. I heard her voice. Saw the hem of her caftan."

"I did too," Grams said, thumping the candlestick on the floor for emphasis.

Of course, that's the stuff magic tricks are made of. I continued tapping and pounding on the inside. Lizzy and Pam did the same on the outside. Nothing.

Grams stomped up and stuck her head inside then announced, "This must be the work of that cult."

WonderDog circled the area sniffing. He wore a stunned look in his dark eyes and a frown over his brow.

I stomped on the floor. "Sounds and feels solid!" I looked at the top again.

In the near-darkness, something gleamed in the seam where it met the back wall. I stood on tiptoe and pulled. Holding it gingerly, I stepped out of the booth.

The light was barely bright enough for me to see—Irma's gold charm—seven small circles linked together—glowed in my hand. Had she intentionally left it for me?

"We have to see what's under this booth! Lizzy and Pam, please help me slide this thing."

As we lined up to push it, Bart Bottom came through the side door to the stage. "Ladies, move that thing at your own risk. It belonged to the Great Silas. We all think it's haunted. That's why it hasn't been moved since the day he died."

Now a ghost on top of cosmic essence, interplanetary travel, illusions, and a vanishing cult leader. I was sick of it. I dealt in reality. "You can tell your attorney we were duly warned."

I put my shoulder to the Vanish Booth. "Let's push."

We moved the booth three feet—the floor beneath it was definitely solid. No trapdoor. But in wrestling with the heavy thing, the back wall sprung open a few inches.

"Aha!" I pointed to the gap. "It had to be! It's a prop for a magic trick."

Pam put her hands on the edge of the moveable wall and pulled. It squealed open another six inches then stopped moving. The wall wasn't so movable. The concealed hinges had frozen after all these years.

I didn't want to believe it but Irma might have truly vanished.

Kal had to get here immediately and do a thorough search for her. Kal! I got another charley horse in my eyebrow. How many things had I done in the last twenty-four hours without keeping him informed?

I took the chicken way out and texted him that Irma was the killer and possibly hiding in the Magician's Hat.

"Okay," I said to the crew, Kal can finish up here. For us, back to Nelson's apartment.

I pried the key off my tender palm.

"Let's see if we can find what this fits."

CHAPTER 37

A guy in a flamingo-printed shirt eyed us as we crossed against the traffic on Central Avenue. "Do you ladies need help?"

"We're fine," I said. "But you should see the other gals."

The hike back to the apartment seemed longer than the mad dash over. Lizzy blotted at her scrapes, Pam rubbed her hip, and WonderDog looked up at us with blank eyes.

We squeezed into the elevator. I pressed six and then reached down and patted WonderDog's head. "You did good, boy!"

The apartment door stood wide open as we had left it.

WonderDog trotted in and began snuffling. We went in the kitchen to cleanse Lizzy's scrapes and ice her ankle and Pam's hip. A few minutes later WonderDog joined us, evidently satisfied that no danger lurked in the apartment.

"Do you think that lunatic is gone for good?" Grams reluctantly placed the candlestick on the kitchen table.

I shrugged. "If Kal doesn't find her, there's no reason for her to return and stand trial. Same with Cosmos. The way Nelson abused

Irma is no excuse for their actions, but they didn't intend for Nelson to die."

Lizzy nodded. "A part of me feels sorry for her but I want her brought to justice."

"It's hard to hide in today's world. Maybe if Irma believes hard enough—then clicks her heels three times while saying 'there's no place like Karma' she might just be able to make it. I don't think Kal will be able to extradite her."

Despite the tension showing on her face, Lizzy laughed.

"The thing is—we have the key. I placed it on the table. "Think. Does this key remind you of anything?"

Pam looked around the kitchen. "Irma and the bald guy tore this place apart searching for a connection. The key is small—stands to reason it fits something small—a tube safe?"

Lizzy closed her eyes, placed her hands over her cheeks, and rubbed the sides of her nose. "I keep thinking about the scented rope. If Irma knew Father at all she knew that he hated the smell of flowers."

"Your father hated flowers?" Little chimes went off in my head.

"The smell bothered him." Lizzy said. "Sometimes he blamed it on allergies."

"And yet he maintained roses on the roof?" I stood up. "Ladies, we begin our hunt in the garden." I pocketed the key.

We trooped up the stairs and out into the roses. Most of the blooms were now withering and gave off the heavy odor of dying flowers. WonderDog tried to help out by watering a couple of them.

"I always wondered why Father kept a garden but never dared ask him. He could have buried a treasure box in anyone of these plots," Lizzy said, waving her arm in an arc. "We could dig up the whole garden but that's going to take forever."

"We have to try."

I looked at the low-rise concrete bunker blending in with the landscaping. A room air conditioner stuck out of one wall.

"Over there." I pointed at the structure. "That's the first place we have to look."

I dashed to the bunker. "It's padlocked." I lifted the lock and let go. It slammed against the hasp with a thud. "I'm not sure about breaking this off even if we had a really heavy hammer."

"That's one big old lock," Grams said. "Never noticed the lock before."

"Grams, that doctor's assistant who called you about Nelson—do you have a friendship with her?"

"Millie? I wouldn't call it a friendship—more like she enjoys a good gossip."

A doctor probably wouldn't have a big hammer in his office but he might have a can of liquid nitrogen to freeze off warts. We can use it to freeze the metal shackle to the point of brittleness. Then I can hit it with a rock and crack it off."

Lizzy, Pam, and Grams stood there with their mouths hanging open.

"There are times when you frighten me," Lizzy said.

"Saw it on television." I nodded at Grams. "My turn to give orders. Fetch a can of liquid nitrogen from that doctor's office."

With a military salute, Grams headed down the stairs, Pam close behind.

WonderDog continued to wander the bushes, occasionally relieving the drought for one of them.

Lizzy and I were left to our worries.

"Once again the shop is unattended," I said. "Not that we could avoid the last few days. But if we get Sophia's endorsement we can't brew cold cream, make soap, and add products to our line without hiring a shop girl."

Lizzy stared at the storage bunker oblivious to me. "Do you

think my father was really that mean? Could he have driven Irma mad? What if there's a body in that shed?"

"Sweetie, your father was a serial monster—not a serial killer. In your wildest imaginings can you see him hauling a body up those stairs? If we get in that bunker we'll be looking for a lock that accepts the small key."

Grams returned followed by Pam carrying a canister. "I showed the doctor's assistant my nursing license and told her it was an emergency."

"And I promised Millie a full accounting of Nelson's murder." Grams looked pleased with herself.

"You can't!" I gave her my best bossy look while reaching for the canister.

Grams smirked. "I'm not going to tell her the truth. Celestial beings and seven spinning planets? They'd have me on senile meds before I could scratch my nose."

"Somebody find a hard rock—not sandstone," I said.

It was too bright out to read the instructions on the canister, but I remembered what I'd seen on that murder mystery show. I turned the canister upside down and sprayed. The air was freezing cold—the blowback of nitrogen fog began to numb my fingers. I dropped the can.

"Look at that ice!" Grams eyes were twice normal size. "That stuff's dangerous."

Lizzy handed me a rock—it was a fairly heavy chunk of white marble with a slightly pointed end.

I struck the frozen lock once and it shattered in three pieces. Continuing to use the rock, I knocked the icy sections to the ground and opened the hasp.

CHAPTER 38

*I*t was cool in the low-slung shed—but not cool enough to store a body. An assortment of garden tools hung from hooks along the left wall. A bag of soil and some clay pots lined the right side. But it was the trunk against the back wall that caught my eye.

Grams stood at my elbow. "That trunk. That was from Nelson's Masked Dangler days."

She trotted across the concrete floor, her excitement overcoming any sense of caution.

I followed her. Lizzy, Pam, and WonderDog crowded into the small space behind me.

With what I'd learned about Nelson, the trunk might be booby-trapped.

Three quick strides and I was at her side. "Let me do this." I gently moved between Grams and the trunk and inspected the lid. I held my breath when I lifted it.

The contents were mostly papers. I moved aside and let Grams have the first look at her son's treasures.

She reached in and grabbed a stack of programs with cover

photos of the Masked Dangler and placed them on the ground. Next came a sweat-stained black and gold bodysuit and a full head mask.

She skipped past magical do-dads, and with a gasp pointed at a brown leather album wrapped in clear plastic and sealed with packing tape.

Grams fell backwards into me.

I held her up. "You okay?"

"It's Nelson's journal—worth a fortune to a blackmailer."

Pam and Lizzy helped her stay on her feet. She stared at the journal lying in the trunk. "It's vile!"

I lifted it out and held it in my hand. "You're certain it's the blackmail book. I have to peel off the plastic wrapper to try the key. Is that okay with you, Grams?"

"Do it out in the sunshine—please?" Grams said with a tremor in her voice.

We went to the patio table. I placed the book in the center. We pulled up chairs and for minutes nobody spoke.

"What would Irma have done with it?" Lizzy asked. "Use it for blackmail? Sell it? What?"

"She wanted money to fund her Seven Planets cult and thought the key held a treasure—money or jewels. I doubt she would have had the time or inclination for blackmail. I'd like to think she wouldn't have exploited the journal but she might have sold it to someone more vicious than Nelson."

I began to peel back the plastic.

WonderDog stuck his pointy snoot onto the table—a low growl coming from his throat.

The plastic and tape had melted together—with gentle prying I was able to peel it away. I took the key from my pocket and inserted it in the lock on the strap that held the book closed.

The key fit. I pulled back the strap and opened the cover. In a large scrawl was written ~ *Property of Nelson Dingler* ~ *For His Eyes Only!*

I hesitated flipping the pages— Pandora's Box.

"We've got to destroy this!" Grams said.

"I don't think it's evidence but we should let Kal make that decision." I slid the book closer to me.

"Olive, please." Grams had tears in her eyes. "I'll never ask you for another thing as long as I live. My son created this evil tool. It's destined to fall into the wrong hands—his wicked legacy will go on!"

Grams grabbed my arm and squeezed. "Please destroy this book!"

Even if Kal found Irma was the journal necessary to charge her? It seemed like just the key would be enough.

"Destroy it?" I stalled trying to decide. "Grams, we might be committing a crime."

"More likely preventing a crime. Think what a professional blackmailer could do with this…thing."

The tears in her milky eyes did me in.

"Okay. There's a barbecue pit in the community area of my condo," I said.

Grams relaxed, the lines in her forehead softening.

"We can take it there and burn it," I said. "If it puts your mind at ease we can hope that any evil attached to the book will be carried away by the sea breeze."

"There are trash bags in the kitchen," Lizzy jumped to her feet, yelping at the pain in her ankle. "Let's cover this thing up and get out of here while we can."

A small part of me wanted to save the book for Kal, but most of me wanted to honor Grams' request. The journal would serve no good and if it found its way into the wrong hands…I thought of all the struggling magicians we'd met in the last few days. They deserved a chance. Even Bart Bottom and Harry Whodunit.

We bagged the journal in a solemn kitchen ceremony. Grams refused to cart the thing in her car so Lizzy and I became keeper of the book of secrets.

"We'll meet you at my condo. We're not allowed to burn anything on the grill except for food, so we'll have to be discreet. The barbeque grill is out back under the sundeck portico."

Pam, Grams, Lizzy, WonderDog and I locked up the apartment and made our way to the bank employees' parking lot.

"Thank you for doing this for Grams," Lizzy said. "She'd never rest easy knowing my father's wicked journal existed. You did a good thing giving her closure."

Lizzy and I arrived at Sandy Shores Towers at two-thirty. We hurried straight to the gas grill and fired it up.

Grams voice cut through the sound of the waves and the cry of the gulls. "We're here!"

I unwrapped the book, peeling off every shred of plastic. "The cover's leather. Should I burn it, too?"

"Burn the whole dang thing!" Grams said. "I don't want a piece of it left."

I scanned the beach and parking area—it looked like we were alone. The balconies didn't provide a straight-on view of the grill area, but just in case I stood away from the building and looked up.

Ivy LaVine, former friend, possible competitor, and guardian of the beaches was out on her balcony. Her apartment was on the fourth floor plus under-building parking made it five stories up—but her angry glare still touched me.

I waved. She didn't respond. Ivy's neighborhood watch was legendary. She'd even reported pigeons for droppings. If she saw dark smoke she'd call the fire department or worse yet, Kal.

"We've been spotted. I'm putting the journal in the flames right now. Step back!"

The pages burned quickly but the leather cover smoldered—dark smoke roiling up to the fourth floor as if drawn there.

"Olive? What's going on?" It was Kal's voice.

As I watched the stinky leather shrivel to ash I tried to decide what expression to use when I turned around to face him—sheepish, snarky, or absent-minded ditz. I'd successfully avoided the officer of law for twenty-four hours and solved a case that would have severely challenged his understanding and friendship.

Grams saved the moment. "Kal, you wouldn't believe the nasty book I caught Olive reading. I'm making her burn it while I watch."

"Don't you ever let me catch you reading such trash again!" Grams said, shooting me a sly wink.

I blushed.

And so, the legacy of the Masked Dangler's journal ended in a curl of black smoke. Irma was on her way to Karma without Nelson's supposed fortune. And Nelson had already dangled a path to his own karma.

EPILOGUE

*S*oap making in my kitchen is always a tight squeeze. The counters were covered with wax paper and two double-boilers steamed on the stove. Lizzy and I were almost back on schedule.

"Kal messaged me today," I said. "That's the first time in the three weeks since the burning on the beach. I guess he's coming around."

"Anything important?"

"Just to tell me a cosmic cult commune vanished from a horse farm outside Ocala. They'd been under scrutiny for years—were considered spacey but harmless."

I lined up the soap molds. "I wonder if it was Irma's cult. She might have found a way to make them all Cosmic Travelers."

"We should've hired her to hypnotize Ivy before she and Myron make a complete muddle of her new business," Lizzy said. "She's planning on calling the shop Macy's South." Lizzy sprinkled a cupful of lemongrass into the melted soap. "She'll get sued for that, right?"

"Yup!" I shook my head. "She won't listen. I've tried to give her some advice but she's still got her knickers in a knot."

Puff tumbled into the kitchen followed by WonderDog. "You two know you can't come in here when we're brewing. Back in the living room you little fuzz balls."

WonderDog poked Puff with his snoot beginning a game of chase.

"I picked Heather up from a birthday party yesterday. One of those over-the-top kids' bashes. Guess who was performing—Harry Whodunit! He does a magical act with a talking rubber chicken."

"Stop!" I almost choked. "You made me spill the goop!" I giggled. "Whodunit has found his calling."

We paused for a good long laugh and then went back to work.

"We need to take Sophia's contract to the lawyer tomorrow. It will be nice to see our Italian friend again. Nonna must be smiling in heaven. Sophia's endorsement of her cold cream would please her no end."

Lizzy began to pour the hot liquid into the molds. "How long is Sophia staying?"

"She said she leased a beachside condo for a month and one for Fabio, too. I don't think I told you but she's had her designer make a few disguises for her—a blonde wig, hats, and sunglasses."

Lizzy chuckled. "She'll not be able to conceal that body of hers or her wiggle-walk."

"Look who's talking about wiggle-walks."

I gently slid a tray of filled molds to the back of the counter. "If those guys from the Golden Aches Spa decide to use our creams we're going to have to expand into a larger kitchen. Funny how suspicious they seemed arriving at our shop in business suits—men of mystery. If only Ivy knew who they were at the time."

"Things always work out for the best," Lizzy said.

"Poshookly?" I giggled.

The End

RECIPE FOR LAVENDER HONEY LEMON SOAP

All natural ingredients! Fun and easy!

This oh-so-soothing soap is Lizzy's personal favorite. You're going to love it!

Supplies:
    Double-boiler pot
    Soap molds
    Wax paper

Ingredients - Order on line:
    2 pounds of organic goats milk soap base
    Dried lavender – crushed in food processor
    1 large lemon
    2 tablespoons of honey
    A teeny touch of grapeseed or coconut oil
    Lavender essential oil
    Lemon essential oil

1. Grate the lemon peel to create lemon zest. Then take out most of the moisture by blotting the zest in a paper towel.
2. Break the soap base into one inch chunks to allow it to melt faster.
3. Put it in the top of a double boiler or a glass bowl set in a pot with about 2 inches of water and set to boil.
4. Stir continuously until the soap is completely melted.
5. Pour melted soap base into a measuring cup for easy pouring.
6. Add crushed lavender (3 tablespoons) Use a whisk to mix all ingredients.
7. Add lemon zest.
8. Add 15 drops of the lavender essential oil.
9. Add 6 drops of the lemon essential oil.
10. Put a thin coating of either grapeseed or coconut oil on a tablespoon (Just enough to coat it. It makes it easier to spoon-out the honey.)
11. Add 2 tablespoons of honey.
12. Mix well.
13. Pour carefully into the molds.
14. Spray alcohol on the soap to remove any bubbles that might form.
15. Let the soap cool completely—usually a couple of hours.
16. Gently remove the soap from the molds.

Enjoy!

Rope is optional.

REVIEWS

WonderDog loves reviews! Please consider posting a review for *Soap on a Rope* and any of the other books in the *Cold Cream Murders* series on Amazon.

For those who follow Barbara Silkstone on **BookBub** WonderDog will send you a virtual slurp.

ABOUT THE AUTHOR

http://www.amazon.com/Barbara-Silkstone/e/B0047L8A8W

To receive an email when a new book is published, or for special sales please sign up for my newsletter. Your information will not be shared with anyone and you may unsubscribe at any time.

https://secondactcafe.com/barbara-silkstone/

"Barbara Silkstone is beyond clever. She's an engaging writer who, with great skill, manages to make her skewed world ring true. The best thing about her characters is that they are not caricatures; they are real with all their dimensions intact. The best thing about Silkstone is that she manages to exhibit equal measures of talent and imagination."

Barbara Silkstone is the author of the COLD CREAM MURDERS cozies, also the *Florence Nightingale Comedy Mystery Series*, light-hearted Victorian mysteries.

Silkstone is also the author of the best selling *Mister Darcy* series of comedic mysteries ~ 9 Books~ plus an additional 10 Regency novels and novellas, all with a light, humorous touch.

Please check out her *Wendy Darlin Comedy Mysteries* – 5 Cozy Capers.

Amazon Author page or
visit her at the https://secondactcafe.com

I love hearing from my readers!
You can reach me on FaceBook, Twitter, and at the Second Act Café

Sign up for my occasional newsletter ~
https://secondactcafe.com

COLD CREAM MURDERS

If you haven't begun to read the series now's your chance!
Glossy Lips – Book 1
My Book

Smokey Eyes – Book 2
My Book

COLD CREAM MURDERS – series

When Olive Peroni put out her family therapy sign, she never thought her top client would be the retired head of a New York crime family. When Olive's nonna dies and leaves her a condo in Florida and a secret recipe for miracle cold cream, Olive grabs the chance at a new life in Starfish Cove, Florida, making designer creams for ladies who spend far too much time at the beach.

But when the quiet little community on the Gulf of Mexico soon begins to compete with a certain notorious coastal village in

Maine, Olive finds herself solving odd-ball murders as often as she soothes wrinkles.

Clean, wholesome, and loaded with laughs!

Each book contains a recipe for homemade cosmetics!

GLOSSY LIPS – BOOK 1

Business is brisk and life is good! Olive Peroni makes a wild new best friend in Lizzy, the real estate agent who handles the transfer of Nonna's condo. When a dead body is found in the trunk of Lizzy's car, Olive despairs that life in Starfish Cove won't be any different than the one she thought she'd escaped. But this time, instead of listening to confessions of murder, Olive's going to have to solve one. Maybe two…

Contains a recipe for Olive & Lizzy's super-creamy homemade lip gloss!

SMOKEY EYES – BOOK 2

Olive and Lizzy's Cold Cream shop on the beach is jumping—business couldn't be better. But when land shark mogul Brent Toast is found floating in the Starfish Cove marina, with his sneer-side up and a knife in his chest, the prime suspect—among his many enemies—is his brassy daughter-in-law. Can Olive & Lizzy save their friend or will this be the end of the *Loud Mouth of the South*?

Contains a recipe for Olive & Lizzy's Smokey Eye Shadow

With love & laugher!
Barbara Silkstone

Made in the USA
Columbia, SC
22 May 2019